W9-BFG-231

Fishbone's Song

Also by Gary Paulsen

Dancing Carl

Dogsong

Hatchet

Sentries

Shelf Life: Stories by the Book

Six Kids and a Stuffed Cat

This Side of Wild

Tracker

Woodsong

Fishbone's Song

GARY PAULSEN

Simon & Schuster Books for Young Readers
New York   London   Toronto   Sydney   New Delhi

If you purchased this book without a cover, you should be aware that this book is stolen property. It was reported as "unsold and destroyed" to the publisher, and neither the author nor the publisher has received any payment for this "stripped book."

SIMON & SCHUSTER BOOKS FOR YOUNG READERS
An imprint of Simon & Schuster Children's Publishing Division
1230 Avenue of the Americas, New York, New York 10020

This book is a work of fiction. Any references to historical events, real people, or real places are used fictitiously. Other names, characters, places, and events are products of the author's imagination, and any resemblance to actual events or places or persons, living or dead, is entirely coincidental.

Text copyright © 2016 by Gary Paulsen
Cover illustration copyright © 2016 by Tim Jessell
All rights reserved, including the right of reproduction in whole or in part in any form.

SIMON & SCHUSTER BOOKS FOR YOUNG READERS is a trademark of Simon & Schuster, Inc.

For information about special discounts for bulk purchases, please contact Simon & Schuster Special Sales at 1-866-506-1949 or business@simonandschuster.com.

The Simon & Schuster Speakers Bureau can bring authors to your live event. For more information or to book an event, contact the Simon & Schuster Speakers Bureau at 1-866-248-3049 or visit our website at www.simonspeakers.com.

Also available in a Simon & Schuster Books for Young Readers hardcover edition

Cover design by Krista Vossen
Interior design by Hilary Zarycky
The text for this book was set in Centennial LT Std.
Manufactured in the United States of America
0817 OFF
First Simon & Schuster Books for Young Readers paperback edition September 2017
2 4 6 8 10 9 7 5 3 1

The Library of Congress has cataloged the hardcover edition as follows:
Names: Paulsen, Gary, author.
Title: Fishbone's song / Gary Paulsen.
Description: First edition. | New York : Simon & Schuster Books for Young Readers, [2016] | Summary: "Deep in the woods, in a rustic cabin, lives an old man and the boy he's raised as his own. This sage old man has taught the boy the power of nature and how to live in it, and more importantly, to respect it. In Fishbone's Song, this boy reminisces about the magic of the man who raised him and the tales that he used to tell—all true, but different each time"—Provided by publisher.
Identifiers: LCCN 2015039684 | ISBN 9781481452267 (hardcover)
ISBN 9781481452281 (eBook)
Subjects: | CYAC: Nature—Fiction. | Self-reliance—Fiction. | Country Life—Fiction. | Storytelling—Fiction. | Old age—Fiction. | Foundlings—Fiction. | BISAC: JUVENILE FICTION / Animals / General. | JUVENILE FICTION / Lifestyles / Country Life. | JUVENILE FICTION / Social Issues / Self-Esteem & Self-Reliance.
Classification: LCC PZ7.P2843 Fis 2016 | DDC [Fic]—dc23
LC record available at https://lccn.loc.gov/2015039684
ISBN 978-1-4814-5227-4 (pbk)

This book is dedicated,

with great love and enormous respect,

to my friend and editor David Gale.

We worked together years ago and now again. . . .

Fishbone's Song

1

Timewhen

Could have been April when this started, this whole business about Fishbone's song, which I 'spose could be called my song just as well. Thing is, I know where it went and sort of how long it lasted.

Or not, maybe it wasn't really April, at least not the way time works here in the woods where we live next to Caddo Creek, just where it spills across three big rocks to make something almost like the homemade music I try to do on the old small guitar I found in the back of the caved-in 'shine shack.

I only know what the time of the day it is so that when Fishbone says:

"It's the time when the willow bark slips enough to cut a thumb's worth and make a high whistle for to blow. . . ." Then I know soon the creek will be swollen from the runoff out of what Fishbone calls ". . . the long mountains," which I've never seen but will someday. And then there will be the little chub fish with the rainbow on their side to net and cut in slits to smoke. And the mushrooms will come soon after the chubs run, mushrooms hiding in the grass like tiny Christmas trees until you see one and then they all seem to jump out at you, and after that to cut and dry them on a slab board in hot sun . . .

When he says that, when he says "time when," it always comes out as one word: "timewhen." Which he says a lot, all the time, about a lot of things. He's old. Very old. So old he can't really be figured in years or regular time and sometimes he'll just say "timewhen" and not follow it up with what he was thinking about. Instead he'll look off at a cloud even if there aren't any clouds in the sky, and smile at some little or big thing only he knows, only he can remember. It might be something as small as a hummingbird hovering on a wild raspberry flower or as big as a war. Same smile. And he might tell you then if you ask him and he might not until later, maybe a year later, when he's sitting on the porch smoothed with 'shine made by the man I've never talked to who brings the clear alcohol in the middle of a night in half-gallon canning jars. Fishbone's old foot will tap his old work boot in a kind of tap shuffle tap, and he'll look off into the place he was then, back then, and he'll tell you in soft words that run together like new honey about what it was; hummingbird or war. Same voice. Same sound.

Nobody knows why they call him Fishbone or even when it might have got started as a name for him. He once said it was because he got a fishbone stuck in his throat and two doctors had to hold him in a half-broken-down wooden chair full of splinters and knots, one holding his mouth open while the second one, who was younger, dug down in his throat with a rusty pair of horseshoe tongs. They pulled out the bone, which came from a big old yellow channel catfish caught off a mudbank, and all he had to ease the pain was two swallows of clear corn moonshine . . .

All the parts of the story tight and told like they were true and they might have been, probably were, the true story. Except that maybe a week later he would tell it different and say that it was when he was fishing for crawfish and had no small hook and had to make one from the backbone of an ugly gar fish he killed in the shallows with a piece of driftwood he used for a club.

And it was not until later, on a still summer night, sitting on the porch listening to the whine of night bugs hitting the water in the dog dish where the moon had come down to sit, that you would find that both stories were true or were thought true . . .

Thoughttrue.

Like timewhen.

All the same, all the same time or place or something happening. No difference in those things because the main part was that it was his name.

Fishbone.

Stories about how I came to be with Fishbone, by him, of him, family to him—all true, all different. All told by the stove in cold times or on the porch on summer evenings while he was sipping 'shine from an old jelly jar or doing what he called "hogging around" in the garden.

First story I heard I was a baby still in birth blood in a wooden beer crate down where the creek crossed under the county firebreak trail. The trail was right on the edge of being a road that sometimes people would use to come into the dark woods, the old woods, for their own reasons, sometimes dark reasons.

Ugly, he said.

Ugly and wrinkled like a baby pink rat and squalling like a hog stuck in a fence. He found me from the noise I made just before a bear got me. Fishbone was working the creek for chubs or maybe a turtle to eat, and he yelled at the bear that was dragging the crate away, and it dropped the crate and ran off, and Fishbone took the crate and me home with him. Was the crate that was in his mind first, he said; it had iron corners bracing good clear pine wood slats that would work just near perfect in back of the stove to hold wood. When he got to it and saw me, saw what it was that had been squalling and screaming, he just took it all home, crate, baby, and all. Thought, he said, that the baby wouldn't last long anyway and he'd bury it when it passed and still have the crate for the back of the stove. Like any other thing that came drifting down the creek that he could find to use.

I was, he said, like Moses in the Bulrushes, drifting down a river . . .

Which sounded made up until I learned to read and found the story in a big leather book. But I still don't know what a bulrush is except it's something to do with water and has nothing to do with bulls. Or me, for all that.

Could have been a tale like the story about his name, about the stuck bone or the small gar fish hook. Especially when you heard the other stories about how he had a second or third or fourth cousin who had a daughter who found herself with a baby she didn't much want or know how to raise. It—*I*, that is—went from cousin to sister to cousin, until finally I came down to being with Fishbone who was already old, so very old, and he didn't have anything to do for the rest of his life except live in a tumbledown cracky-shack in the woods, and so I had a home.

Third story was I was left with a note in a cardboard box on a church step. The God man who found me there knew somebody from the family that took in kids, and they knew somebody else who could take a kid, but none of them could have any more kids to care for. I wound up with a state woman who looked for blood family and that brought her, finally, to Fishbone, and since we come from some same kind of family blood, I was given to him.

To raise.

And other stories about being found where fairy families had left me under the side of a night-glowing old stump in a shallow hole. Fishbone was looped on 'shine and since he could feel and see things of mystery when he was on 'shine, he saw me there, in the glow from the stump. He took me home thinking I was witched and could see things ahead and maybe bring him good luck, like a piece of clear rock candy or a double yolk egg when you crack it in the pan. If the yolks don't break before they fry . . .

All mixed stories and seemed to be made up except:

Except.

In back of the stove is the wooden beer crate with good pine slat sides and steel-braced corners and some old stains that might have been left by my birth blood.

And.

When they come to get me and made me go to school for a year and a little more until they knew I could never fit in, had some big words about how I could never fit in and brought me back to live with Fishbone, with my family, but in the meantime taught me to read. Right there, right then, I saw an old letter from the state said they would send a little check to Fishbone once a month to raise me in a "goodly manner."

And.

When I came on being maybe ten or eleven or twelve years in the world, I was hunting of an evening for either a fox squirrel or a grouse because Fishbone had a feeling he wanted to eat one or the other and I came into a gulley and there it was . . .

A stump, a fairy stump where I could have been put down in a small hole as a new baby by the woods people, the night woods people, their stump, glowing blue-green in the new dark so pretty it almost had a sound, a blue-green sound I tried to make on the guitar as part of his song, Fishbone's song. And you take that along with finding that I sometimes see things ahead—like I can know, absolutely *know* for certain if a squirrel is on the other side of a tree even without seeing him. Know enough to make the sound, the "chukker" sound that will bring his head around the side for the one clear shot so you don't ruin any meat with the bullet and you kill him with the brain shot so very sudden the death smell, the gut smell, won't taint the stew. All without seeing the squirrel first, just knowing it's there.

So then true, all the stories about how I came to be with Fishbone were true, or could be true, thought true.

Thoughttrue.

Or maybe none of them.

But there was the wood box, and the letter from the state, and the glowing stump, and me, there I was, and Fishbone, and the woods, and the creek. So who can say which is real or not completely quite?

And Fishbone's song, his first song, with a hum at first and then the words all coming in an up-and-down roll to match the old boot tapping and sliding on the porch boards to make time, and a soft shuffle sound like the boot was dancing and drumming at the same time.

First Song: Witching Boy

Witching boy,

in the night,

in the night.

Witching boy,

brings the light,

brings the light.

For everyone to see,

and know,

Witching boy,

brings the glow,

of life.

Shine on, shine on, Witching boy.

2

Newtime

No memories of living at first . . .

   Just clouds of pictures and thoughts that might have been, probably were, like music you can almost hear and think you hear, but it's not almost really there. Fuzzy. Until the state came and took me when I was small and then taught me to read, I didn't have anything but picture memories.

   They worked, the way Fishbone's stories—his songs—worked. I would see something, like a red berry bush, but I didn't know colors, how to say or think colors, and Fishbone would say things that worked, but only for someone who knew some things.

I didn't know some things. I didn't know how anything was said. He'd say something was the same color as the bottom stripe on the side of a creek chub, or that a panther scream was a caterwaul coming on like two men fighting with barbwire whips and hard words . . .

I didn't know yellow-blue, which was the bottom stripe on a creek chub, or that what panther-cats did when they got to talking was really to give out a screech that made the hair come up on the back of your neck. And on that was the fact that I'm old now, either ten or eleven or twelve, maybe thirteen summers, and I have never seen men fight each other, especially with barbwire whips and hard words.

Haven't seen any other men, period, as far as that goes, except for once a month when the man from the state comes to check on things and brings a big box of what Fishbone calls "fixins" to make food—flour, bacon, salt, sugar, coffee, now and then a jar of pickled beets or small cucumber pickles some church group puts in the box because, Fishbone says, it makes them feel like good people. I like the good people pickles, kind of sweet and sour at the same time, but don't like the beets because they make you pee red and I don't like that. To pee red. Fishbone says for me to eat a slice a day just the same because he says it has iron in it, but I can't see any trace of iron in the beets or the pickling juice. Plus I had a small magnet I found in a box of junk in the attic, or sort of an attic, and it didn't stick to a beet slice and so that was that.

No iron.

Oh, one other man we see, or sort of see now and then, is the man that comes sometimes on a dark night to leave a jar or two of moonshine. I stayed up one night and got a look at him. Fishbone leaves a few small bills or silver change from what he calls his war money because he fought in a place called Korea and got shot some. That's how he says it: "I got shot some, there in a place called Korea, and they've sent me money since." The man with the box of fixins brings the money once a month when he comes to check on us. Or on me, I think. And then Fishbone leaves a little money on the side of the porch in an empty 'shine jar when the other man comes in the night with new 'shine.

He looks just about like Fishbone, far as I could tell in the dark: old, with a hacked-down beard. Except he might move a little easier than Fishbone, who moves slow, and now and then has a left limp. I asked him once if the limp was because he got shot some in the place called Korea, but he just looked off at the sky and had that smile. Soft smile. Like he was remembering something good, which didn't make sense if you're thinking about getting shot some.

Only one time he talked about it was when he drank over half a jar of 'shine sitting in the rocker on the porch and told the story-song about the first time he had what he called deep love, book love, magazine love, going to marry her forever love, for sure and true love. But. The army come and took him to go to the place called Korea, where he said he liked to froze to death, was never so cold. So cold that when he got shot, some of the blood froze on the way out and plugged the holes in him so he didn't bleed out and kept him alive just long enough. Just long enough for them to throw him across the hood of a jeep bouncing down a frozen road, tied down with two other men who were already dead and frozen stiff. Heard the bullets hitting the frozen bodies. Just long enough to get him to a doctor who fixed the holes in him. Just long enough for him to get back across the ocean in a plane, and find his first deep love that he thought would last forever had up and taken to a new man who hadn't gotten shot some in the place called Korea.

His story-songs were like going up a stairway or a ladder where at the ground there was just a touch of something you knew would be good, and if you waited and climbed it, there would be something good at the top.

His best story-songs, the ones where he went in his thinking to the small smiles and looking off into the clouds, came when he sat in the chair and drank half a jar of 'shine. Didn't last long. Like burning a candle at the top of that ladder. Get up there, get the good story, then the 'shine would be too much, and the candle would burn out, and he would get quiet again, looking off into private places until his old eyes closed on the memories and he would sleep.

Sit there and snore, Old Blue dog next to the chair sleeping with him, sleeping like he'd been poured onto and into the porch, snoring the same exact sound as Fishbone. Like he'd been drinking 'shine with Fishbone. Thing is, he wasn't old. Had three dogs since I came, or maybe four, coming on five, all flop-eared, drooling hounds so full of love they'd come up and put their head under your hand to feel like they were being petted, move their head back and forth for the feeling.

Every one named Old Blue. Fishbone said all hounds had to be named that. Old Blue. Because of a song that had a line that said, "Old Blue, you good dog, you." Named right off, as soon as they came to us—and that's what happened; they just came to us. They'd show up all covered with mud and tick and fly bites and move in, and as soon as they were there, they'd get next to Fishbone and stick there like they'd been there all their lives, act all old and tired, and sleep next to Fishbone and the rocker unless I went to go hunting. Then they'd jump up and hit out of the front of the cabin like they were on fire.

They were good to go with if you watched them, watched and listened to them and knew how they acted, and that would tell you things. Where an animal might be, and what kind of animal it was;

one sound if they saw a squirrel, another sound—
almost like a bell—if they treed a coon or bear, and
just howled murder if they saw and chased a deer.

I asked Fishbone once where they came from
when they just showed up, and he said God sent
them, said God made them in the forest out of
spare parts of other animals, leftovers, and that's
why they were so floppy and loose skinned, and
they roamed the woods until they saw a place they
liked and they moved in and sat down. Of course
I knew that people used them, hunted with them,
and that sometimes they ran and got so far they
didn't come back; that's how the people lost them.
They'd start to run a deer and go so far and fast
they wound up belonging to us.

Or maybe I should say they came and laid down.
Next to the rocker, sleeping when Fishbone sipped
'shine and did his word-songs, and they went to
getting fed scraps and cooked guts from fish and
animals I hunted, which we mixed with boiled

rice. Went to getting fed and petted. Fishbone said it was the onliest true love there is in the world, the way a dog loved, unless you found the right woman, which he thought he did twice. But was wrong. Or he said some had the true love of Jesus, but he wasn't one of them, though he thought maybe that was as good as the dogs' love. Clean, he said, clear and clean and no chains holding. I sat by a tree for a time one afternoon in the sun with Old Blue number three with his head in my lap and wondered if I had the true love of Jesus but no feeling came, and I thought maybe you had to be older, or know more. Maybe later, I figured, when Jesus got to know me better or I got to know him. Fishbone said He was everywhere and that if I listened to him when he sat in the rocker and talked and learned about things, it all might come to me. Or might not. He said it had not come to him, the true love, either with a woman or Jesus, but it was still there, out there, for the lucky ones.

In the meantime he said the love from a dog would help me to understand about it.

Love.

I'm not sure when I started to learn things from Fishbone. Might have been right away when I came to him, however that happened. I can't remember much from the first times except that when I was, I think, three or four, he taught me how to pee off the porch on the downwind side so it wouldn't splatter back on my legs, and to use the outhouse and magazine paper to wipe, because if I did it again in the yard, the dog would eat it and lick my mouth afterward and give me worms in the butt. I don't know if all that is just perfectly true, but every dog we've had has licked my mouth if he caught me off guard, so I figured it wasn't worth taking a chance. I don't want worms in my butt.

After that first learning that I can remember, things kind of came so fast it was all I could do to catch up.

First the woods. The old cabin we lived in was just barely not the woods, made out of old slab boards left from a sawmill some place far off and long ago. Weathered and gray, and according to Fishbone, older than him, and so full of gaps, he said you could throw a cat through the wall without hurting it. So I asked him kind of snotty, did he ever throw a cat through a wall, because when I was young and didn't understand how his story-songs worked, I was kind of snotty, or as he said, I was part of a know-it-all. And he had a look he gave me that had no smile in it when he thought I was being part of a know-it-all. And since it was the only time he looked even a little cross or sideways at me, I stopped being that way every chance I got.

So I was already in the woods, more or less, sleeping in the cabin with the night sounds and the bugs all part of me, and it was just natural to fold into it like it was home, my bed, my warm green woods bed.

Second Song: Devil Love

She found my heart,

and took it.

Found my soul,

and shook it.

Found my song,

and spoke it.

Found my life,

and broke it.

Dance on, devil woman.

Dance on, devil love.

3

Woodstime

I was never afraid of the woods.

Never felt out of place the way you can be with people, schools, crowds, ratchety noise—the way it was when the state came to take me and put me in those places with those things and people. Had to fight sometimes. Had a big fight with a boy twice my size, beat me all to hell and gone, just for being different. He thought because I was down I was done, but I got up and clipped him with my thick mail-order boots, and he went to puking and left me alone after that.

Still didn't like it. Even when they opened my

brain and put in good things. Taught me to read. The little school was in a hill town and had one old computer which I never got to use, or even learned how to use. Boy in the school said that he knew of a place where they had more, many computers, and they could play games on them and talk all over the world on them, but I wasn't sure he was telling the truth; he also said he had an uncle who could dead-lift six hundred and ninety pounds with one hand, so believing him was a stretch.

But this little school with bad ceilings and a leaky roof had books. A whole room full of books on shelves, and an old woman who had soft blue hair and wore glasses on a cord around her neck who was in charge of the books, and she thought you should read them. No, that's not quite right. She loved the books, and when she touched them, it was like she was petting them, and she taught me how to read, made me read, made me want to read, made me love to read. Did it all in two months and twenty-six days, which was all I was in that place until they sent me on back to Fishbone.

In the shack.

In the woods.

But the old woman with the glasses on a cord around her neck and hair that smelled blue didn't forget me. Every month when the man from the state came with bullet money from Fishbone getting shot some in Korea, and kid money so I could be "raised in a goodly manner," and grocery fixins, the old woman sent one or two books on up with him. I'd send back any books I'd read and we'd trade back and forth.

History books, poetry books, western books, nature books, even some by an English writer named Shakespeare. Poems that didn't rhyme and were hard to read until I found they were supposed to be a play, and if you said the words out loud, they made more sense. Sometimes made you feel new about some things.

Old Blue numbers three and four both thought I was crazy when I came to spouting Shakespeare poems that didn't rhyme off the porch, but Fishbone seemed to like them. Didn't say so, but closed his eyes and smiled and nodded and shuffled his feet the way he did when he was doing his own songs his own self. Word-songs. Same smile, and even bigger when Shakespeare came to working on love talk.

He must have known about the woods. Shakespeare. To have all those words rumbling around and to be able to bring them out in the way he did, the dance of them, he must have known how it was in the woods.

How green and still it could be, and how it could smell and sound so that it was inside you, part of you.

Could be the best part of you.

Like home. Like my home.

I folded into the woods not long after I learned

about using the outhouse and peeing on the down-wind side of the porch. I remember walking off the porch and down to the creek and sitting on the sand at the side of the clear, rippling water, and putting my hand in and seeing the way it wiggled my fingers, made them look all wavy.

Everything else disappeared. Just gone, clean and gone like there was never anything else. Just the woods. From that day on every chance I got—and that was all the time—I went into the trees. I'd take just one step in, move to the left and then right around a tree, and I was there: Home. Moving quiet, like a knife through water. Warm, green, leafy light all around me, sounds of birds all before and after me, in the woods. *In* the woods . . .

First just to look. But by the time I was six, I started in to hunting with Fishbone rules. Fishbone had a way to do everything, all things—way to think, way to cook, way to see, way to live, way to be.

And his hunting rules were simple.

If you killed it, you had to eat it. You could eat it raw or you could eat it cold or you could eat it cooked, but if you killed something, you had to use it for food.

I learned that when I started. I made a small spear out of cane, sharpened it to a needle point with the kitchen knife, and worked down the creek bank looking for anything that moved. I was thinking of crayfish but couldn't find any, so I tried spearing some chubs flashing in the shallows, but they were too fast for me. Downstream a little more I found and speared a frog. Not a big bullfrog like we later got out of the swamp one hill over. You could fry the legs, big as chicken drumsticks almost, wrapped in flour or cracker crumbs, legs jumping and twitching in the pan as they fried, and tasting good, completely good, when they were done and crisp, sprinkled with salt.

This first frog was small. Come shooting off the

bank like he was shot from a spring, went underwater and stopped. Just stopped in clear water wasn't four inches deep. I poked the cane spear down and got him, pinned him to the bottom, killed him. Then I reached down and grabbed him with my free hand, and took him back up to the cabin to show Fishbone.

Good, he nodded. Now eat him.

The frog, I asked.

Yes, boy, he said. You killed it, you eat it.

The whole frog, I asked, thinking I don't believe I can get the whole frog down and hold it, guts and skin and all. Thought of the tongue, sticky and kind of long, and it almost made me puke but he shook his head.

On frogs just the back legs, he said, cut them off and wash them in the creek and bring them in and fry them in a little bacon grease until they crackle, then eat them.

But I said there aren't two bites. No meat at all.

Then you shouldn't have killed it.

Lessons learned. Don't pee into the wind, don't get worms in your butt, and if you kill something, you had to eat it. I had to cut the legs off the body of the frog. Bright green and shiny skin with black spots, cut them off just where they joined the little body, then wash them clean and dust them with flour, same as with a big frog.

Looked so small. Little spindly legs hardly big enough to see sitting in the pan. Then scoop bacon grease out of the can by the sink where we pour it after we cook bacon. Solid and gray-brown, two spoons tastes all salty and bacony.

Then outside to pick up the axe and split wood for the cook stove. Big axe, double-bladed Collins almost impossible for a six-year-old to pick up, and then worse to have to swing it, again and again, to split enough wood for a hot fire; then carry it in, light the fire, get the stove hot, put the pan with grease and tiny frog legs over the hottest part, and fry them until they stop jumping and jerking and twitching, until they crackle.

Then eat them. One bite. And all the time thinking you'd done something wrong. Bad wrong.

By killing one small frog.

And then back to the woods.

Only knowing more now, this time, knowing that hunting is not just to kill. Hunting is watching. Watching to know. Watching to learn to see and know and learn. A way to get food, but more, more than that a way to learn, to know. A way to be.

A hunter.

A watcher.

The spear was not enough, not fast enough for chubs. Once in a great while we would stretch an old seining net across a part of the creek down where it pools and net twenty or so to salt and smoke. They tasted good smoked, smoky and oily and salty. Each fish was about the length of Fishbone's hand spread out, with fat and slick and oily meat. But he didn't like to net them too often because he said we would take them all out with the net and not have any fish. But any I could catch alone we could cook in the pan and have with sliced potatoes, picking the meat carefully off the bones.

But they didn't bite. I tried with some line and a small hook I found in an old box in the shanty shed at the rear of the cabin. Dug a few worms and hung the line off an old piece of willow and they came to it. You could see them gather around bait. But they just nibbled and nibbled at the worm until it was all taken off, broken away from the hook.

So I couldn't spear them and we only netted them almost never, and they didn't take a hook, and you can, I figured, get hungry something awful just watching and learning about things but never taking any food. Well, true fact is there is always food here from what the man brings once a month when he comes to check on things. Can always make biscuits and gravy with flour and bacon grease and lord only knows how many cans of beans there are stored in shelves in back of the stove. And cans of some meat called Spam. Fishbone said he lived through some hard times when he was small, where the onliest thing he had to eat were lard sandwiches on week-old bread. With a little salt. Said sometimes his mother would find a way to buy flour and yeast and make bread or biscuits to have with gravy. Burned brown gravy made from flour and lard usually on the week-old bread from the bakery. Penny a loaf, he said, and they couldn't afford that. Lard and old bread. Three times a day. So now he kept cans of beans and some Spam. Just in case, he said, just in case it came on hard times again, but he wouldn't use any of it unless it happened. Hard times. I couldn't just open a can of beans or Spam whenever I felt a little lean in the belly, he said. Go out, he said. Earn it.

So I needed a faster way to hunt and I thought on it and decided that I could make a bow and use cane arrows—straight and light—if I could find the right wood for the bow. I tried elm, using an old leather bootlace for a string first, but it either bent too much and was too weak, or if thicker wouldn't bend at all. Messed around with other wood I didn't know the name of and finally settled on dried willow. There was a stand of old dead and dried water willows that grew when there was a heavy runoff from the long mountains one year, then no runoff again, so they died and stayed there, straight and clean from knots or splits. I picked a piece a little thinner than my wrist and whittled on it with the kitchen knife until it was rough tapered. Then Fishbone showed me how to scrape and shave wood with a piece of broken jar glass from the junk pile where it seemed like we threw stuff away until we needed to use it again.

Bow was about as long as me. I read in one of the books all about a crook a long time ago named Robin Hood. Was really good with a bow. Said he could shoot one arrow into a target and then another so it split the first arrow down the middle, but I found later that there probably wasn't a man like him, that it was all based on an old tombstone behind a church in England that said:

Here lies Robyn Hode

'Nere was an archer so giud

Period. There never was any more about him anywhere, but people started making up stories about him based on the tombstone. There was nothing else you could hang on to as true about the whole business. Good. Fun to read. Only made up.

But in the book they said a wooden bow cut and trimmed to the right shape was called a stave and that's what I had. A stave. Until I cut notches in the ends for string and hooked them up with the leather lace. I shortened the string until when I held the bow in the middle, the string was back away from the center of the bow about the distance of my spread hand. Cutting, tapering, and shaving was slow, but I'd sit of an evening with the oil lamp flickering in the soft night air moving through the slats in the walls and listen to Fishbone tell his song-stories, sipping his 'shine from the jar and making word pictures in my head.

Something made them slide in there, the song-tales. Slide into my brain so they seemed alive, real inside me in some way so I could almost hear the colors, smell the sound.

Sing-song stories of old times, sad songs of the hard times and lard sandwiches and wearing one pair of Oshkosh bibs until they were more patches than bibs, all-over wear-holes and fixed with pieces of cotton flour sacks. And baby sister wearing pull-over shift dresses made from the same flour sacks. And patches on them as well, so many she had a nickname of that: Patches. Same baby sister dying of the croup, of the coughing croup hacking so long and deep you could hear-feel it in your whole body every time she coughed, night after night, day after day, until finally the end of it, the end of it. The end of her coughing and the end of her, of Patches. Buried wrapped in an old piece of binder canvas with the wooden slats still riveted to it. Shiny brass rivet heads against the straw-polished old wood strips. Buried in the same flour-sack shift dress, buried with a handful of wildflowers held in her hands, wildflowers she loved to pick and smell. Buried in a hand-dug grave by the back of the house. Buried forever. Buried.

Sad songs. So sad he had tears, not 'shine tears but real ones when he told it. Sang it with the foot-shuffle beat on the porch boards and old voice cracking, thinking of burying her. Patches. Had blue eyes, and red-blond hair, and a smile all the time, and they were all buried with her. Part of the song. Blue eyes and hair and smile. All buried.

Arrows were easier. The bow had a nice snap to it, not heavy to pull but zippy. The string made a thrumming sound, lower than the bottom string on the old guitar when I plucked it good and taut. And cane from along the creek bank down where it edged the swamp was dry and light. I cut five of them a little longer than my arm and on the front end carved a point as sharp as a needle. On the rear end I gouged out a shallow notch for the bowstring, and by pinching the end of the arrow shaft with my fingers, I could pull it back over a foot. Not all the way back to the cheek or the chin but a good way toward them. From eight or ten feet away on the mud side bank of the creek, the cane stuck in nice. Solid. In about a hand width. I tried a farther shot or two, but without feathers on the shaft, the arrow tended to head off sideways and I couldn't hit anything even close to what I aimed at.

But for then, for a seven- or six- or eight-year-old boy who was just starting to hunt, it was good enough, and I started working the creek for chubs. They would sit on the bottom, or near the bottom, with their nose up into the current, and the water only a foot or two deep, clear as glass. Just sit there, holding themselves in place, and I picked one, leaned out so I was almost over him, not three or four feet away, pulled the bow—I could almost taste him dusted in flour and cooking in the bacon grease—aimed carefully . . .

And missed.

Shot over his back a good foot and the cane arrow stuck in the bottom. Or almost stuck. The bottom was gravel and mud, mixed, and the arrow hit a stone and broke.

But I had another arrow. Had four of them. And there were chubs all over the creek bottom and I stepped barefoot out into the water, closer and closer to another one, just holding his place, leaned over, drew the bow . . .

And missed again.

And broke another arrow.

This time I heard a snort and turned to see Fishbone sitting in his rocker on the porch, watching me, his shoulders shaking, and I saw he was laughing. Almost to himself except that now and then he would make that snort and he took a sip of 'shine and said water bends things.

What do you mean, I asked.

Bends things you look at. Bends where things are, bends what you see, bends how you see.

But I can see the chubs right there. They're right there in front of me.

No they're not, not like you see them. They're lower than they look. Try aiming just below one, like you were going to shoot under him.

Sounded silly but Fishbone almost never said anything silly. Or wrong. Or wasted. Never seemed to waste a word or a thought. Didn't talk much but when he did, when he did, it was better to listen. So I waded in the shallows near the bank in the soft mud squirting up between my toes, found another chub, leaned over, guess-aimed the width of my hand below him, and let go.

Missed again. But closer this time, much closer, so that the cane shaft almost rubbed against him on the way by, and he jerked away to the center of the creek into deeper water. Fishbone said, did you hit him, and I said no, but so close I might have got a scale.

I was down to one cane arrow, which was not a problem because the bank was filled with cane and it was easy to cut with the kitchen knife.

Another fish was sitting there in the shallows, and I moved and stood near and almost over him. I'd seen the big herons and other hunting birds go after fish and frogs the same way. Just stand and stand without moving, without even twitching. Watching, waiting, waiting until the fish or frog had almost forgotten they were there. Had gone back to just being a fish or frog, just being what they were . . .

And then strike.

Sharp beak down, swift and down and through them. Hardly ever missed, almost no splash, and almost never missed. Then up, flip the frog or fish up in the air, and catch it and swallow, zip and gone.

I drew the arrow when the chub was still, had forgotten I was there—I could have been a tree trunk—drew it back slowly, so slowly, aimed at the bottom edge of the chub, and released, clean and gone. The needle-sharp point of the cane caught him halfway up his side just in back of the gills and pinned him to the bottom.

Got him, I said to Fishbone, and I held him down, wiggling, with the arrow, and reached down the shaft, took him in my hand and said, again, got him clean.

Good, he said from the porch. That's one for me, now get one for yourself and we'll wrap them in flour and slice up some potatoes and melt a mite of grease and we'll have a good bite of food before dark. When the stove is hot, we'll make a pot of coffee and have hot coffee sipped through sugar lumps for dessert.

He loved sugar lumps. Not a lot of them but now and again a lump of sugar between his gums, and he'd suck coffee through it. Said it settled his guts. Sometimes he'd do the same thing drinking 'shine. Just hold a sugar lump there in his gums and sipped the 'shine right through it. Never said if it settled his guts that way, but he sure liked it. He'd let me have coffee with water to thin it down the same way, through a sugar lump. Said I was too small to drink straight stove coffee the way he made it and no 'shine at all. Once when I was being the worst part of a know-it-all and he wasn't looking, or maybe was and let me do it as another lesson on how it wasn't good to be a smart mouth—once I drank a full cup of strong coffee through a sugar lump held in my teeth and I was up all night and must have peed ten times. I think I was six then or maybe seven or five. Didn't like it much and I have never tried it with 'shine. Tried that sip of 'shine plain one time, just enough to touch my tongue, and it burned so bad I thought my mouth was on fire. Still don't see how Fishbone can sit there and sip it steady from a jar like he does and it never seems to hurt him much. I did that and it would turn my brain to mush. 'Course I'm still young, maybe ten or eleven or twelve depending on which true story about how I came to be with Fishbone. Maybe you had to be older to take the 'shine and strong coffee even when they're sucked through a sugar lump.

Didn't seem to hurt him much, the 'shine—mouth or brain or body—but then he's old; old, he says, as dirt. That may be why. Like leather or hard wood or rust iron. Just plain tough.

But it sure makes his songs come easier. The 'shine.

Third Song: Barefoot Blues
Two-dollar shoes,
                two-dollar shoes.
Pinch my toes, make me sing the blues.

Can't do nothing,

> but moan and wail.

Man come along and throw me in jail.

All for stealing,

> them two-dollar shoes.

Can't do nothing but sing them blues.

4

Stovesmoke

Sometimes it was not hunting and it was more like going into something. Something you knew. Something you wore like part of you, like the trees and grass and the water in the creek and ponds and the brush were your clothes, your skin. You. It was all you.

Tried to tell Fishbone about it, how it felt now that I had come into it, knew more about it. At first I thought it didn't go in his thinking. He smiled a bit. No teeth smile; had his eyes closed like he was seeing something in there, in his thinking, and hadn't heard a word I said.

But I was wrong. Usually I was. Wrong. When it came to thinking that I was out ahead of Fishbone, I was almost always wrong.

It can all be like that, he said, everything about you, your life, what you do, what you did, what you're going to do. Everything you see, feel, hear—everything you do. Everything you are. Your life, all your life you'll wear it, he said, if you do it right, right in how you see and know your own right, know it in how you think yourself.

Everything, all that you are or ever going to be, will be like a cloak, he said and smiled—just as a cloak of many colors.

Arrows.

I got a little older, eight and up a bit, or maybe nine and up, and I came to where I could make them better, so they'd fly better and not turn all sideways. I was working near the bog swamp just down from the shack, looking for crayfish or bigger

bullfrogs, and I found two big shypoke wings, a left
and right, with the big end feathers still stuck on
them. Fishbone said there were other names for
the birds, big swamp birds that had long sharp
beaks and ate frogs and small fish and now and
then a small snake. Called them herons, he said,
some people, and white ones were called egrets,
but he said he had never heard them called anything but shypoke. Just lying there in the water-
grass, the wing ends. One out to either side so you
could almost see the big bird between them except
it was gone. Head, guts, bones, legs—all gone.
Small tracks around them, around the wings, like
an Old Blue hound only much smaller. Maybe half
the size of my palm where the Old Blue hounds
made a track in soft water-grass or creek mud bigger than my whole hand. More than not a fox, red
or gray, caught the bird and killed him to carry off,
but the wings were too much to handle, so the fox
took them off and left them.

Feathers. In books. In one of them I came to see an old drawing of some men who ran with Robin Hood—just in the story of him, not for real—and they had arrow holders on their backs called quivers and in the drawing each arrow in the quiver had feathers on it.

So I had the feathers from the shypoke wings and I wasn't sure what they would do for the arrow, but every drawing showing arrows in the book showed them with feathers on the back end. There had to be something to them. And I had my cane arrows from the creek side. So all I needed to do was figure out how to put the feathers on the arrow.

Not so easy. I could see the feathers had a center line and they would split easy on the line with a little pressure from a knife. So I had feathers with a soft vane sticking up off a flat bottom, and I sat by the lamp of an evening with a cane arrow and a piece of flat-bottomed feather and wondered how it could be attached. Wasn't any glue or tape in the whole cabin. I had tried splitting a cane shaft and sliding the feather in the slit, but it flew out when I shot . . .

Thread, Fishbone said. Take thread from the sewing box, split the feather with thread wound around the arrow and through little splits in the feather, do two feathers opposite each other, and tie the thread off with double knots. Make the feathers about as long as your finger and they'll fly clean. True.

How do you know that, I asked, and he said that's how the Apaches did it.

How do you know what the Apaches did, I asked, which put me on the edge of being the worst part of being a know-it-all since I was not even fairly sure I knew what an Apache was supposed to be. Didn't find out until I was some older and the lady who sent books sent me one about American natives of the Southwest. They were a tribe of Native Americans who were so tough it took a whole army to stop them. But I didn't know that when Fishbone said they did arrows with thread holding the feathers on, and I asked him again, how do you know that?

But his eyes closed until only a little edge of white showed, and he smiled, and seemed to look off the way he did when he was moving around in his memories. His foot started to shuffle-pat the floor, and I knew he was gone. Or I thought he was gone, gone away to that other place, except that he got that dreamy look and smiled with his gums and said, stovesmoke.

A word, one word that way, and I said, what's that? What's stovesmoke?

The way you move, he said, the way you move in the woods through the trees like a knife through water, like fog, like the smoke from the stove on a damp morning, all low and sliding through the trees.

Being.

Watched you from the porch, low and sliding like smoke, all of it closing in back of you like you wasn't there, wasn't ever there before or after.

Like smoke.

Like stovesmoke.

Sometimes I didn't know if Fishbone even saw me. Mostly his eyes seemed closed while he was swimming in his mind. As far as noticing me, watching me move through the trees from the porch, I would have bet he didn't see me much at all.

Was a time, he said, was a time when Jimmy Applecore showed up. Once long ago, and then again later. He moved like that. Always moved like stovesmoke. Even sitting at a table playing poker, he was like smoke, there and not there. Jimmy drank fancy 'shine. Sweet moonshine and old bourbon, so he stayed just under the cloud all the time.

Except after Korea. That's when the guv'ment treated him like a show pony. Sent him around to places where people had money. Used him to make nice about being a soldier. A hero for his country so rich people would give money to the guv'ment men walking Jimmy around, same as if he was on a rope.

'Til some man tell Jimmy he was lying about how he held a machine gun up in his hands to fire it even though he had the burn scars from the gun to prove it. Jimmy didn't say nuthin', just threw an apple from a bowl on the stage down into the audience so hard it knocked the man out, made the apple explode so there wasn't nothing left but core. That's how he got the name Jimmy Applecore. Prouder of the apple than he was of the medal. Didn't hold on to the medal, but he carried the apple-throwing picture from the newspaper in his wallet.

Met Jimmy when I was waiting to get patched up from being shot some in Korea. Took one look at me—bloody, puking, swearing—and he said he knew where there was a place in the ocean near Florida where the guv'ment dumped a whole barge full of new jeeps and trucks just to get rid of them. Dumped them in water only fifty feet deep, and he knew where to get a diving suit and an old boat to borrow, and we could get rich, he said, clean rich. I said how and he said tires. All the tires were new, made of pure rubber with good tubes, and full of air, so if we unscrewed the nuts holding them, they'd float up.

Slick, Jimmy said. Slick as nose snot on a glass doorknob. It was like finding money, he told me, and wasn't even stealing it. Guv'ment threw them all away so people would buy new cars and tires and not just use the old jeeps and trucks, and it all worked like Jimmy said. Took turns wearing the diving suit down, down in the blue, just popping the tires loose and letting them shoot up.

Like stovesmoke, Fishbone said. Life going just that way, just as smoke through the trees.

Everything working just exactly right. Just as Jimmy said, Fishbone said. Slick, and we did all the tires we could get to, pop and up, and only a little bother from sharks coming in closer and closer until you jammed their noses with a screwdriver and they'd jerk and wheel away, and then money. And more money. Money for pockets and extra money to keep down in the boot. More money than there ever was for us, good money, better money than ever was for Jimmy to buy a '49 Ford with a big V8 motor almost new. Almost new. And fast. Snap your neck fast, crack your shoulders fast, screaming fast, lay rubber in two gears fast, so fast, so fast . . .

So fast it took Jimmy out of all the rest of his life. Everything gone. Had met a woman, not just a whiskey woman but a woman he was going to marry and live with and have his life with, and he took her for a ride in the car, the hot car, the '49 Ford with the big engine.

Charlene with him in the car, fast in the car, beer

drunk in the car but not whiskey drunk in the car, and it didn't matter. Just the beer took Jimmy and Charlene, moving at a hundred miles and more in one hour, off the side of a bridge from loose gravel into a dirt embankment so hard, so hard . . .

Jimmy Applecore was an Apache from out west. Went through the place called Korea with Fishbone, tied Fishbone on the hood of the jeep between the two frozen dead men so he didn't die in the ice there, die in the cold there, saved Fishbone so he could live the rest of his life even though Jimmy couldn't. Didn't. Didn't have any more life after the dirt embankment.

You couldn't tell, Fishbone said, you couldn't tell where Jimmy and Charlene ended and the '49 Ford began, all mixed in the dirt of the embankment. Gone. Gone same as the sister in the flour-sack shift dress wrapped in the binder canvas. Gone like the croup took them. Gone like the frozen two men on the hood of the jeep. Dead.

Gone.

But Jimmy had an old arrow. Warped piece of wood with a stone head and dried-up crackly feathers. Carried it all through Korea and drinking and diving for the tires and the end with the '49 Ford, carried it wrapped in a piece of oiled soft deerskin leather, wrapped and tied with oiled leather thongs.

Said it was his Medicine Arrow. Said it was from old, way old times, when all they had was stone arrowheads to hunt with, to live with, to be with. To be. And when Fishbone said he thought Jimmy was lying, when they were both drunk one night in a canvas tent in the army, said he thought Jimmy maybe carved the arrow shaft himself, Jimmy had just smiled. Held it out, held the arrow out, and said touch it. See it. Feel it. And you'll know, you'll feel-know how it is, how it was and will always be, and when Fishbone touched the arrow, it felt warm, seemed to send a warmness into him, through his hand.

It is for the path, the path from the old ones, from before measured time, before White Time, before the path the old ones have made for us to follow in our lives. And after life, Jimmy told Fishbone, tells of the one true path we are all to take, shows us the way. The stone head of the arrow will show the way, point the one true way of the spirit road if you believe, believe in the magic of the arrow path.

Believe.

And Fishbone said he knew it then, knew that it was true and that he believed that it would work for Jimmy, and when Jimmy and Charlene hit the embankment and entered onto their journey on the spirit path, he knew, Fishbone knew, that the arrow would show them the way.

After that the arrow was gone, disappeared, at least as far as Fishbone was aware, but he had seen it, seen the arrow and how it was made, how the feathers were tied on with thread wrapped through them, and so I did the same, the same as Fishbone showed me.

I split and tied the shypoke feathers, cut short pieces of them, on the back of the cane arrows just ahead of where the bowstring took the shaft. And when I fired the bow, the arrows quit turning sideways, followed a path, a true path to the hunk of soft dirt I used for a practice target.

So I could shoot longer now, a little farther, with a little more accuracy, and I cut a new willow and dried it for a stronger bow and became at least part of what Fishbone had said of me, became like stovesmoke. Moving.

In a way . . .

In a way I moved . . .

In a way I moved out of the cabin and became even more a part of the trees, the leaves, the grass, all of everything that was all of the woods. I circled, bigger and bigger circles out away from the cabin, away from Fishbone, away from what I was, what I had been, and I became something . . . else. More. Something more and something better and something new. New.

But not away in my thinking. Not really away from Fishbone in my thinking because I ended each circle, at the end of each day, hunting, seeing, learning, each day when the sun came down slower, came down at the end time, the closing time. Each day I wound up back at the cabin. Back with Fishbone, where I could tell him things I had seen and done and he could tell me the same. Things he had seen and done.

Things to see . . .

From me, things to see.

Early morning, barely dawn, and I came on a small pond in a clearing. Perfect. Perfectly round with grass edges, and I slid my bare feet down through the wet grass, felt it between my toes and stopped, and there she was, a small doe. On the other side of the pond, taking a drink, raising her head as I was there, seeing me but not running.

Just standing. Still. And I was still. Sunlight just coming over the pond to catch her standing there. Her head raised and two drops of water left her lips and fell. Fell almost in slow time, fell back into the pond, where they made two perfect circles of ripples that looked like jewels.

Perfect jewels. Round jewel-ripples spreading out in light and she stared at me forever, forever after in my mind, a picture that filled my brain and would always be there, always be part of my thinking.

I could taste her, smell-taste her. She was meat and I was a hunter now, and forever after a hunter, and I could smell-taste her on the sides of my tongue, in my breath, but I could not shoot. Wrong shot, wrong arrows. Just cane sharpened to points with no blades, not good enough, no sharp edges to cut and not strong enough for bigger animals and so, no. Not this time. No shot. But still there for me, still tasting her and always after caught in my mind-taste-smell so I owned her even as she turned and walked back into the trees. She was mine.

Always would be mine.

Always.

Always I would be a hunter moving like stove-smoke, and always in all ways she would be mine. To bring up and see and taste and smell. All ways.

And I told Fishbone about it that evening. Sitting on the porch in the lamplight I tried to tell him that when I was hunting and came upon the deer by the pond, even though I couldn't shoot her, couldn't make the kill, still she was mine because I had seen-smelled-felt-tasted her, knew her, *knew* her and would always know her. And he told me of his second Forever Woman that came after the first Forever Woman who left him while he was in Korea getting shot some.

A second Forever Woman who stole his heart

away, stole his soul away, and left him broken and open inside.

But never was.

Never was his second Forever Woman at all. Same as I never shot the doe, that doe, same as.

Name of Judith Eve.

Story about Judith Eve.

But stories, he said, are never just stories alone by themselves.

Shuffle-pat, shuffle-pat, the old shoes on the worn porch boards, worn and polished.

Shuffle-pat, shuffle-pat, and a sip of 'shine. Worn boards making an almost-sound of their own. Like a baby drum. Babydrum, babydrum, shuffle-pat, shuffle-pat . . .

Stories are like old cedar shingles on a good roof, Fishbone said. They happen, they look good, but they won't work. Roof will leak. Has to be other shingles, overlapping, one shingle overlapping the next to make the roof to not leak, to make the rain flow over and not through, to make the story. Make the story flow.

Same as.

Same as stories, he said. Story won't stand alone, can't stand alone, has to overlap other stories, has to be overlapped by another story.

Name of Judith Eve was the second Forever Woman who never was, never became but would always be.

Judith Eve.

But not alone. She didn't just happen, didn't just be there out of nothing. Had to come from other stories, other places. Had to have overlap stories.

Had to come from cars.

Fast cars and white lightning. Same as moonshine, 'shine, used to be called white lightning, made back up and in the hills, back in dark hollows and kept in crocks and jars and wooden barrels.

Old-time people brought the ways from other countries, over there in Europe, Scotland, back in places, and came to the dark hills here, and started stills and made more whiskey from corn and wheat than ever was before. Even to old George Washington, who had a set of stills, made thirty thousand gallons in one year, they said, and then had the guv'ment put a tax on the other whiskey, on all the hill people whiskey, so they couldn't compete with him.

Tried.

Tried to use the army to get the taxes. Tried to use the army to stop other people from making 'shine. Tried to make it illegal and finally did.

Made it wrong for other people to make 'shine.

All right for him. Just all right for him and the other rich ones, the big ones.

But against the written law of the whole country for anybody else, stomped in by the army, same army as won the war, the Revolutionary War, same army that fought eight years to make us all free, all except women and black people and native people and poor people. They didn't get to be free, no matter what they said or did. Had to take it for themselves. Had to come down out of the hills and take it all or never be free. Had to roll on down and take it, make their own whiskey and sell it in the dark. Never free. Never open.

But all the rest, all the rich ones and white ones, they were free.

All free except those who wanted to make their own 'shine and put it in barrels and use it for to barter or buy or live.

All illegal. All illegal then and kept illegal on down, year after year, same law, same illegal all the way down, and had a war about it. Had a war in the hills, called it the Whiskey War, just stomping down on anybody wanted to make his own 'shine, and the army won it. Won the whiskey rebellion.

Made it so it was still illegal, and then came Fishbone and Jimmy. Took the tires off the sunken barges and had money for pockets and more, so much there was enough to hide down in your boot, so much that Jimmy bought the '49 Ford and took Charlene into the embankment when he was beer drunk to start their journey on the spirit path.

So much money from the diving on tires that Fishbone, he bought his own car. Same kind, same as, '49 Ford two-door coupe with the big V8 motor, and he learned to mechanic some. Found a way to put a blower, a supercharger, off an airplane over the carburetor to blow down a jet of air with the gas, made the car wild fast, wicked fast. So powerful it would just sit and shred the tires if he up and tromped on it.

Crazy car.

And he got to talking to a man over in South Carolina, and the man told him there was a place where a man with a wicked fast car could make even more money, more than what he could even stick in his boot if he wanted.

Wanted to.

Wanted to put an iron tank in the trunk of the car, fifty-gallon iron tank, and fill it with white lightning, fill it with moonshine, fill it with 'shine and take it north to another town where they would put it in bottles and add some tea and gunpowder for color and sell the bottles with fancy labels. Call it bonded whiskey. Call it rich man's whiskey even though it's made by a poor man. If he wanted to do all that, he could make five dollars a gallon.

Two hundred and fifty dollars.

For each trip.

When a man in a factory slaved hard for thirty-three dollars a week, worked till he dropped every day for thirty-three dollars for a six-day week, Fishbone could make two hundred and fifty dollars for a trip that didn't take four hours.

If.

If the revenuers waiting on the road in their own cars didn't catch him, didn't stop him, didn't shoot him, or burn him down, or wreck him.

If.

The money was there.

If . . .

So Fishbone did that thing. Put a tank in the trunk of his car, and beefed up the rear springs to take the weight of the tank, and put thick truck tires on the rims so they wouldn't shred with the speed and load, and started up those roads at night with a tank full of white lightning.

Thunder Road, they called it.

Thunder Road.

Not for weather, but because the drivers of the cars back then could let the exhaust out ahead of the muffler to get more power. That last bit of speed. Caused a roar that near made your ears bleed, couldn't hear for two days later even with cotton shoved in your ears. Crazy, wicked crazy speed. Cars meant to do eighty miles an hour were pushed to a hundred, then one twenty, and over one thirty.

Always running on moonless nights, leaving at midnight and boring a screaming, roaring hole through the pitch dark, running so fast they like to run over their own headlights, running so fast they outran the gunfire when they barreled through road-blocks, running so fast that it was impossible to do.

But they did it. Fishbone said they did it. Fishbone said he did it, said he couldn't not do it, had to do it.

Had to.

Lord god, he said, they had to do it because of why? Because of the money, one thing. Money as crazy as the speed, more money than any of them had ever seen, money that kept rolling in, but more. More to it than just money.

Changed them.

It all changed them. Some of them country boys, some of them fought in wars, some of them not, some of them could read, some not, some knew a lot, some didn't.

Some were all different until.

Until.

Until they drove the white lightning road, the Thunder Road, in impossibly hot cars. Fords, Chevrolets, even a Cadillac or two. Basic cars turned into wild things.

Like turning a housecat into a cougar, Fishbone said. Same animal, in a way, but really not even close to the same. Radiators blowing, seals exploding and covering the roads with oil, axles warping, windshields shattering, wrecks with bodies turned to paste, and all of them, all of them fighting to take the next load up the road.

Crazy, Fishbone said. It was that they were crazy, but all crazy in the same way, all crazy with the money that they never saved, crazy with the speed of it all. Everybody lived in either shacks or old trailers, stuck back in the brush off the main road, muddy ruts for driveways with a shed for working on the cars. And out in front of the sheds, a spare motor either hanging on an A-frame made out of logs or a tree limb, and somebody always, always working on a motor if he wasn't on a run. Or hadn't been caught and sent to federal prison.

Come a day now and then, or two or three days, when there wasn't any white lightning to move, to transport, Fishbone said you'd think they'd take some down time. Take some self time and relax. But no.

No.

Instead they all headed south down into Florida, where there was a flat place to run, down to Daytona Beach, and they'd race the cars with empty 'shine tanks, race against each other— those that weren't in jail or prison—race without seat belts or helmets, race the crazy-wicked fast cars for money on a barrel head, all the money, all the money they made running the 'shine north, screaming fast on the beach and drinking beer and sometimes moonshine and fighting and sometimes dying there in wrecks.

And so to Judith Eve.

Fishbone's second Forever Woman.

Never called her Judy. Never called her Eve.

Always called her Judith Eve. Lady, he said, like no other lady ever lived. She'd come down to the races with Bobby J. Never knew his full name. Just Bobby J. Won most of the races with a cut-down-and-built-back-up '53 Ford. Had some kind of wild engine in it that would outrun anything but light, and he'd show up with Judith Eve in the car with him, set her aside on the crude bleachers they had put together out of planks for local audiences that always showed up to bet on the cars.

She'd sit . . . perfect.

It was not just that she was pretty, or beautiful. Thick brown hair that fell to her waist in back. Shined like it had glow heat in it. Huge brown eyes, tipped up at the corners just that touch, always on the edge of smiling, and when she laughed, it sounded like silver bells back in a deep forest. Hear it and you had to laugh with her even if you didn't know what she was laughing about.

Body, Fishbone said, that would make a grown man like buttermilk, and when I asked him what that meant, he said I would know later. Maybe a lot later because I still haven't figured it out. She wore white T-shirts and shorts, he said, and after racing in the day they would have kegs of beer in stock tanks full of ice and drink beer and argue about the racing and sometimes fight. There would be music from car radios set on country stations, three or four cars set on the same one so it could be loud, and they would drink and fight and dance on the beach.

But not Judith Eve.

She'd sit and sip a beer and talk and smile and laugh and just be . . . perfect. Not tangled up in all the mess of racing and fighting. Just come down

with Bobby J and go back with him and say hey to
other men. Never with them, just to them. Say hey.

Said hey to Fishbone.

That was it. All of it. Fishbone was young then,
which was hard to believe. That he'd ever been
young. And shy. Bobby J was above him, had the
best car, was the most, the very most of it all. Black
hair in an Elvis cut and combed back in a ducktail,
Levis with the belt loops cut out, T-shirt with a ciga-
rette pack rolled up in the sleeve, black leather engi-
neer boots with a strap and buckle. Looked like
they all wanted to look, drove like they all wanted
to drive, fought like they all wanted to fight.

Until.

Until he got caught by revenuers who laid a
welded spike strip across the highway and blew all
four of his tires when he had a full tank of lightning,
clocking somewhere just above a hundred miles an
hour, boring a hole through the night. Spun him
sideways, and around twice, and then it rolled him,

and he lit up like a shooting star when the gas and lightning blew and there wasn't anything left of Bobby J.

Not a thing.

But Fishbone had gone on by that time. Had wrecked his own car the same way only not as bad. Blew his tires too, the revenuers, with a spike strip, but with Fishbone only three tires blew and he slewed off the road and into the brush, and only half rolled once, and didn't blow. Just started to drip and burned like a fire, and he got out in time, though his leg was broken. Left leg. Why he limped a bit. He was still young then, and the judge took some pity on him, and he did some time, but not in a federal prison. Only four months in the county jail, which was how long it took his leg to heal anyway, and he got out of jail with a healed leg and no money. None. They took it all, what he had left. Didn't let him keep more than sixteen cents and a matchbook with a bar name in New Orleans. So he moved on, he said. Thumbed his way back south to New Orleans and took a job sweeping and mopping out flop houses and juke joints and bars and the like. Dark houses, those places, houses called the Rising Sun in songs. Man named Bobby only with no J owned the bar and the flop houses, and gave him a cot in one of the flops, with only just enough money to live on. Barely. If he had had to pay, it would have been fifty cents a night for an eight-hour shift in a cot, hot bunking. While it was all rough, rough trade and tough people, men and women seemed to be mostly made out of scars, he found he didn't mind it much. Coming from jail where the only food he got was mashed sweet potatoes, one dry hard biscuit, and a cup of black coffee mixed with grounds so strong you almost had to chew it, one time each day, coming from that the red beans and rice he got for a quarter each day, with a cup of soft ginger beer three times a day, was fine.

He thought a lot about the cars. Fast, wild, crazy

cars. And he missed them and knew he would own more cars, drive more of them, but never again running 'shine or racing them the same wild way. It's not that he grew up so much as that he grew out. Thought wider. Thought longer. Didn't just see the sunset but thought about where it came from; like a fighter who hits not just to the point but aims a foot past it. Tries to carry the hit longer, make more of it. Saw everything that way.

Called it stock car racing later. Said it all started then—what became national automobile racing. Stock car racing. But there wasn't anything stock about the races he was in, the roads he drove. The cars were so far from stock they almost didn't qualify for the brand name. Fords in those days weren't really Fords. More like a skeleton of a Ford with a monster put inside it. Cars that ate meat, ate men.

Still later when they stopped running white lightning and just raced, he watched their names in the papers, heard talk about them on radios, heard how they raced and how many of them died in fiery wrecks and what was called "devastating collisions."

But he had moved on.

Still he never forgot about Judith Eve and how she would sit on the end of the bleachers. Sit there just exactly right. Brown hair falling down, eyes tipped up a bit at the corners, lips like the red of life, body . . . body arched and taking the sun so it seemed the light came from inside her. Sat there just exactly right.

Perfect.

And he loved her still in his mind the way she had been then. Didn't try to look her up or write to her or know more about her or see what had happened to her. Owned her in his thinking, knew her in his thinking, was with her in his thinking, would always be with her in his thinking.

Like me with the doe standing by the pond with the jewels of water going out and out. I would own, would see her, know her all the rest of my life.

Fourth Song: The Long Road

Burning, burning,

up the long, long road.

Burning, burning,

up the long, long road.

Never knowing day by day,

whether to swear or whether to pray.

Moonshine makes a heavy load,

up the long, wrong road.

5

Greenroom

Fishbone has a lot of rules where he makes things right in your head, but some of them you don't understand at first.

If you kill it, you eat it.

Don't think about bad things if you don't want bad things to happen.

If you think something is red, it's red.

If you think about something small a lot of the time, it will get bigger, but if you think about something big, a lot of the time it will still get bigger. Like fish. Or debt.

A house is something to keep things out, not to

keep things in. Like weather. And biting flies. And some snakes.

Always stay hungry. It makes you see things better. Especially if you're hunting. Or trying to think up a new idea. Orville and Wilbur Wright were always hungry when they were working on how to fly. Stayed in a shed, Fishbone said, with slab walls, and had eggs to cook and eat, eggs in a board shelf with a hole for each egg, and every egg was numbered. Number said when it was laid, told how fresh it was. That was hunger, Fishbone said—fat, full people don't number eggs. Just eat them. Anybody who numbers his eggs is hungry. All the time. When I asked how he knew about Orville and Wilbur and their eggs, he looked at me like I was going to be the big part of a wise guy and then shrugged and smiled and said he saw it in a magazine picture of the inside of their shack. Was still true, even if Fishbone wasn't there to count the eggs himself.

A room is as big as you want it to be in your head.

And there it was. A change had started in me just before that about the room. Not the same change as later but a change. The thing is, what with one thing and another, it seemed like everything was changing for me. On me. About me. Don't know how old I was because I never quite knew when I was born. Might have been twelve, plus a little. Fat side of twelve. But I'd taken to having dreams I didn't understand about families I'd never had, about girls I'd never known, about parts of girls I'd never seen. About parts.

About.

Dumb dreams.

But I couldn't seem to stop them and one evening on the porch I told Fishbone about them. About the dreams and he said, what else?

What else what, I asked.

What else would you dream about? Comes a

time, comes a time when you've never had a car and your voice is changing. What else are you going to dream about? Came to me, came to me later than you because I never knew peace until I was older. Still young when I went to Korea and got shot some and then cars and running white lightning up that damn road and never knowing time for real dreaming until later, older, when I was in New Orleans swamping out the flops and juke joints, and then it was all there, all there in flat light night and day for to see and smell and feel. Touch. Couldn't dream. Didn't dare to dream. Too real.

Too real.

Remember one woman, lady, one lady named Clair. Called herself C. Just that, C. Hard to say if she was pretty or not. She was . . . everything. And nothing. Hit your eyes, your brain, your breath like a storm. Worked in one of the houses he cleaned and sold everything about herself. Sold what she was for what you had. All that she was for all that you had. Used to sit and play soft music on a guitar, everything propped on top of the guitar. Had a snake tattooed around her neck. The tattooed snake ran down the center of her chest, down and down and you didn't see where it was going unless you were someone else. He never saw where it went. They said she used to have a live snake there, around her neck and down, but it died so she had the tattoo done.

Once you'd seen C, Fishbone said, there was no more dreaming about cars or families or girls or parts of things. It was all real. Too real for dreaming. Now go and fetch cool water from the creek and make nighttime coffee so it will be there cold in the morning to wash the night taste out of our mouths.

And I did.

And that night I dreamed about rooms. Or a room. My room. And how big it was getting to be.

I slept in one corner of the cabin behind a short

wall that came out from the sidewall of the cabin. Not a room so much as a slot. Fishbone slept on the other side of the cabin in the same kind of slot. I slept on an old strap-iron cot just wide enough for one person with iron ends that were decorated with little designs so it looked like the little posts that held up the ends of the bed were stuck in a kind of flower. Fishbone said the cot belonged to an old Confederate soldier from the Civil War name of Season, or maybe Ceesen. He never spelled it. Said the old soldier died in the cot when he was over a hundred years old and he was alone and they didn't find the body for going on a week. Not here but in another cabin-shack. During a warm summer month. And the body went off, he said, as bodies and other meat does when it's warm, so after they found him and buried him in a rubber sack—Fishbone said it was before they had plastic— nobody wanted anything to do with any of the old soldier's stuff. Said it smelled too bad. So they burned the shack with all his stuff in it. Bed too. Fishbone came along later, maybe a year later, and the bed was still there, standing in the ashes, only rusted a little after the fire took off the finish a bit. But all there, springs and all. And the stink was gone. Burned away.

Fishbone took it home, never one to waste anything. Still had the box he might have found me in when I was a baby. Still had old work boots so worn they were falling to pieces. Said he might need the leather from the tops to fix other things that wore out or were broke, the way cowboys who were rustling cattle in the old days sewed old boot tops together to make pouches to carry cartridges on the side of their saddles. I had used the sleeve of an old canvas jacket to make a quiver to hold arrows, held up with a piece of clothesline rope over my shoulder, so I understood how he could have taken the cot. Used the cot.

He slept on it for twenty years, was still sleeping

on it when he found or got me. Kept me in a box on the floor. Same box he might have found me in. Or not. And when I got too big to sleep in the box, he had another cot, a little bigger, and he put me in the old soldier's bed and moved to the other one.

Still the same.

Still the same now. Box in back of the stove with my baby stains in it to hold stove wood. Probably never be moved again. Old boots in the corner by the door. The same. Old coats hanging on nails, just the same.

But the dreams changed. I dreamed of my room first as it was, and then out, out and out and wider, until it was bigger and bigger, outside the cabin, outside and out until it was all of everything. All of it—all I could see and be in—all felt like my room. My own room, my own place to be. To be.

Told Fishbone about it, about the dream, and for a few minutes he looked at me, like he was studying on something. And maybe not something he liked much. Like when he talked about getting shot some in Korea. Then he leaned back in the rocker and closed his eyes.

Thought at first you were a familiar, he said.

What's a familiar, I asked.

Witching thing, he said.

I don't understand.

Don't suspect that you do. Don't suspect on it at all. There's a lot of things you don't understand. It's because you're young. Ain't had time to understand a lot of things, being young and all.

I waited. It was the only way with him. It never helped to push on a thing. You had to wait for an answer. Problem was, sometimes you had to wait a long time. Might be he'd answer right away, might be in an hour when he took some 'shine, might be tomorrow. Might be never, like some of the questions I asked him about women. Grown women. And what it was that made a man think on them so much. He never did answer. Just looked off into away and sipped 'shine and smiled. Dozing, he said, dozing on his memories. Some you might like to get shed of, wear them off, burn them. But now and again a memory was so fine you wanted to keep it. Like a warm cloud you could doze on. Just sit in the chair, and sip on a jar of good 'shine and close your eyes and doze on the memory. Part of getting old, he said. Maybe the best part of getting old.

This time wasn't so long. Took a sip of 'shine from the jar, really just a lip wetter, said you came three ways. In a box, from family and guv'ment, and from a witching stump. Can't pick one because they're all the right way at different times. After you were here with me and learned to suck a milk rag, then a calf bottle, one night I took you to a ghost stump glowing in the dark, and put you on the ground to see if you were a familiar. See if the light jumped from the stump into you. It was on a cold night, soft cold, and you caterwauled some.

Sounded like an old hog stuck in a gate. Might have been the cold. You were partial to being warm when you were small, and I maybe had a bit too much 'shine in me that night. Wasn't so good at controlling it then, like I am now. So I held the blanket open a bit to see if the light jumped into you, but it didn't. It didn't. You just got cold and let out more noise. So you ain't. Ain't a familiar.

Again I thought. Again. What's a familiar, I said. Or who?

They help witches work when it comes to casting spells. Sometimes be a little boy, sometimes a little girl, sometimes a cat, and now and again just a candle. Lit, of course. Candle won't work unless it's lit. And it helps if it's a beeswax candle or tallow. Not store wax.

You believe in all that, I said. Witches and the like.

There are things we don't understand to know. To know. And maybe if we don't know about how a thing is, how it works, how it can be—just because we don't know how it is doesn't mean it's not real.

And so there are witches, I said.

Maybe. Maybe not. I've never seen one, known one, but I've heard. Heard things that don't make a lot of sense. Knew an old lady once, could touch her elbow and tell you if it's going to rain. Tell you when. To the hour. Some can take a willow fork and walk around and tell you if there's water and how deep down it is. Seen that many times. The stick bends down when they find water. Sometimes bends down so hard it strips the bark off in the man's hand. They call it witching water, or divining water, but I don't know if they're witches or not. Just know I don't understand it. And I can't do it.

And I'm not one. I can't hold a stick and find water.

No, no. He shook his head, sipped his 'shine. No. And you ain't a familiar either, or it would have showed by now. But you have these dreams, thick dreams, that don't make a lot of sense, except. Except they do, they kind of do make sense. They come from thinking of things, thinking of things around you, and I think that just means you can see. See out and around and front and back. See new and old things. You dream-see your cot, your sleeping place, your living place, going out and out. Getting bigger, and I think it means you are more, want more.

So what do I do, I asked.

Was me, he said, smiling that soft, no-tooth smile. Was me, I'd go out and out and see where it led to. Go find the edge of the dream.

And so I did.

Took the bow and a sleeve-quiver with a half-dozen cane arrows and forty or fifty strike-anywhere wooden matches, what Fishbone called Lucifer fire sticks, and an old steel pot with a bent handle, and at the last minute a small role of stovepipe wire I found on a nail on the back of the cabin. Fishbone had talked of making small rabbit and squirrel snares with the wire, and I had a thought of trying it.

Also took a small paper pouch of wheat flour and corn flour mixed. Maybe two cups worth.

Didn't know where I would go or for sure why. Was just going to go, go see. Go and do. What Fishbone said. Go to the edge of the dream, wherever that turned out to be, and even starting loose that way, nothing hard in my thinking. Even that way, I found myself hunting. It was that I couldn't not hunt, if that makes any sense at all. I could walk in the woods, could think I was just walking in the woods along the creek, where I started, but inside of four steps I was hunting. Looking deep in the water, not just at the surface, looking deep in the creek for fish or crayfish or big leopard frogs. Looking not just at the bushes on the shore or out ahead of me, but looking inside, deep into each bush, looking for that line or motion that didn't belong, wasn't part of the natural line or motion. Studying tree limbs for a jerk or twitch or shape that wasn't part of the limb, part of the tree. Might be a grouse or a squirrel on a tree limb, or a grouse or a rabbit on the ground. A sound that didn't fit, a line that didn't fit, wasn't part of the natural line or sound. Might be alive. Might be, might be . . . something.

Might be food.

And even not to kill.

Not yet.

Not to kill everything or even anything. Later, later, but not yet, not now. Just moving, moving through and around and of the woods and trees and brush and water, fitting in, making myself part of that natural line, natural sound, natural feeling.

Hunting.

To see and feel and know the woods. Moving out to the edge, to the edge of what there is to know, to know more, understand more, see more, learn more.

Hunting.

To know. To learn. To see and feel and hear and look inside, inside of everything you see. Not just the surface of the water, but deep down into it; not just the squirrel or the rabbit or the grouse but inside it, inside to where you know, know the arrow will hit and will kill and will make food where there was no food.

To the edge of all you know.

To hunt.

To be a hunter. To see the edge of your dream, go right to the edge of your dream and then through it. Through the edge of all you know and think and into the next thing, the next part.

I moved along the creek down past three big bends it made around small hills, barely rises in ground. And on the moss sides of the hills, the north side, I found some mushrooms, some morels, and I picked them and put them in the pouch with the flour for later. Little Christmas trees is how they looked and was the only kind of mushroom Fishbone said was always safe. Easy to see. Easy to know.

Where the creek hit the swamp where I had found the shypoke feathers that I used for the arrows, it made a sharp turn to the left, and it was this bend that marked the farthest I had ever gone from the cabin. I'm not sure of distance, but if a person walking slow while watching, hunting, made maybe a mile an hour, then it was close on a mile from the cabin.

The longest away. Here—if I came this far—I usually headed in a big circle to the right, skirting the edge of the swamp and working back around to the cabin in a great loop through the woods. That's when I was hunting, strictly hunting for food for the cabin, either squirrel or rabbit or grouse. And usually I took something in that circle. Or got a good shot at something. And just what distance I had gone so far I had seen plenty of game—several rabbits, a couple of grouse, one opossum, and big leopard frogs in the creek. All close. One grouse was on a freeze and stood so still I had to walk around him. Or her. Couldn't tell from looking at it. I could have almost grabbed it and if we're telling the truth, I was tempted. Grouse boiled in fresh creek water with morels thrown in made a great soup. And my backbone was steady moving toward my stomach, as Fishbone said when he was hungry. And more truth, I was always hungry. It seemed. I could just eat. And eat.

But.

I was moving. Hunting. Not killing yet. So I passed over the easy kills I saw and kept moving, moving. I went off to the left of the swamp throughout the morning, off to the left and then the land started to rise. First in a gentle slope and then steeper and steeper until I was moving onto a ridge made of a large gray rock outcropping that stood out like the backbone of some giant animal skeleton. I worked along this ridge, not on top because I had learned that all things look to the top of a ridge or a hill and I didn't want to scare away animals that might be in the same area.

Below the ridge line and slow, two, three steps, pause, stop, study what's ahead, start again, stop right away, and study, study, breathe in slow and out more slowly, wait, wait.

Two more steps, stop. Think of fitting, fitting in to the ridge line, into the grass under my feet. Think of being the weather, air, all of everything. Fit in to the edge, edge of the dream. Slow. Sloooow. Looking for a line, a curve that doesn't belong, doesn't fit.

Down the face of the ridge moving that way, watching, seeing, but more, more, feeling, *feeling* everything, feeling all things, knowing all things. Closer to the creek where it wound around the side of the ridge, water against the rock, cutting away until it left a small clearing back against the rock face and out to the creek, with thick brush and grass coming down to the water on the other side of the creek.

And there.

Right . . . exactly . . . *there*.

A grouse. Sitting low in the grass. Body down, head up a bit. Frozen. No motion.

Slowly draw the arrow back, feel where it's going, how it's going to go and then without thinking about it, release. Soft "thrumm" of the string and the cane arrow is gone, clean and gone, hitting the grouse just below the head, through the neck.

One flop.

And done. Dead.

Food.

I had an old two-bladed pocketknife that Fishbone had given me, only one blade, the other broken off, and I used it to cut the bird's head off and the lower part of the legs and feet. Then tore the skin away—easier to skin than to eat feathers because they never all come off when you try to pluck them—and then a small fire, creek water in the pot with the whole grouse. Small bird. And the mushrooms to let them boil until the meat falls off the bone. Gather more wood while it's cooking, all night wood, then before dark set a trap for crayfish.

The creek is alive with them and the tails taste almost sweet. Fishbone says they taste like lobster, or shrimp. I don't know. Wouldn't know. Never tasted them. But crayfish make your mouth water just thinking of them. Well. So does grouse. Or rabbit. Or biscuits and flour gravy. Or anything.

Fishbone says most people eat the tail and the guts, but I could never get into scooping the guts out and eating them, so I stick to the tails. Don't eat rabbit guts. Don't eat squirrel guts. Don't eat frog guts. Don't eat guts.

Just the heart. Sometimes. Throw it in the stew as I did with the grouse heart. Just meat. Good meat.

Where the creek curved away from the little

clearing, the bottom was almost free of weeds and grass from the current picking up speed around the corner. On the side of the bank there was a U-shaped gouge that came back into the dirt about two feet. The water in the U was about five inches deep with a clear, sandy bottom. I took flat rocks from the ridge stone and made a small underwater wall across the face of the U and left a two-inch opening in the center. In the back of the U I put the grouse guts, head, feet, and feathers, except for the outer wing feathers that I saved to use on cane arrows later, and I weighted the guts down with stone. Kept the good parts on the bottom. Meat, skin, guts bring all the scavengers in—fish, crayfish, even leeches, which will come if the water is still. Leeches don't do very well in fast current. Which is just as well because I don't want to eat a leech.

I figure through the night some shiners might come in, and crayfish, and I could sneak down in the morning and cover the front of the trap and have a hot breakfast with what I catch in the night. I also took some of the wire and made a snare over a rabbit trail that tunneled back into the grass. About a four-inch loop, a half inch off the ground and straight across the little packed trail, tied off to a small ash tree on the side. All the way Fishbone said to do it.

Then more wood for the fire, and still more. The grouse stew bubbled away until the meat fell away from the bone and the mushrooms were soft, and I drank the stew water and ate the grouse and mushrooms, and put the leftover skeleton and bone bits with the bait in the water trap.

Pulled a bunch of leaves back against the rock wall for a bed, the fire kicking heat in under the ledge, warm around me, nestled back in and closed my eyes.

But no sleep.

Not yet. Questions kept popping up. How, I thought.

How.

How did I know what I knew, how to hunt, how to move, how to work a ridge, how to be, how to . . . everything?

How to hunt.

How to be a hunter. A knower. A learner. A person who sees things. Not just to kill. That was part of it. But not only that. Not just to kill but to hunt. How could I know that?

And I knew. Fire flickering, heat coming back into me, dark in the woods around and I knew, knew what it was, how it happened. It wasn't me. I was just a place that it came to, came through.

It was Fishbone.

It was his stories, his shuffle-pat story-songs that came into me as whole ways of being, knowing. Came into me like heat from the fire, came in to say one thing, maybe about fast cars or running 'shine, but it would work for all things. Work for thinking, make thinking better, so it would make me more whole, make me think smarter and better about everything I was, everything I did.

Don't know if he meant it.

I think he did. I think he knew what he was doing with all of it, his thinking, the rhythm of his thoughts and voice. Maybe the way he smiled. Sipped 'shine. Way he looked away just when he should look away, answer just when he should answer.

Make me think just when I need to think. Do. Feel. Be. Give me an answer when I need one. Straight out. Hold back when he didn't think I needed one.

What with the grouse and mushroom stew, I was full as a tick and feeling dozy, so I pulled back in the leaves and went to fast sleep. No dream. Or at least not one I could remember. But it was summer just when it was warmest, before it turned into early fall, and later at night when the fire went down and out and the night air came in and found me it cooled some, a little, and I started to wake up. But I pulled in more leaves, brought them up and over me and went back to sleep until splashing nearby woke me again when it was full light.

It was two shiner chub fish fighting each other over the grouse guts inside the box trap. I jumped up, kept low, found a small flat rock I had put down the night before, and used it to close the gate on the trap, penning in the two chubs. I also saw that there were three medium-size crayfish in the trap as well, and when I looked down the stream bank, I found I had snared a cottontail rabbit to add to the food supply. The rabbit had stuck his head through the noose of wire, wrapped twice around the small trunk of the ash willow, and was dead, choked out.

I made a fire, and when it was going, I went off from the creek to take care of what Fishbone called "my necessaries." Then I went back and cleaned the chubs, putting the guts back in the creek for the crayfish to eat. I put the chubs and the crayfish—the

crayfish without cleaning, but whole—in the breakfast soup. While they were boiling up, I took the rabbit from the snare, removed the wire, and cleaned
him as well, also putting his guts in the creek except
for the heart, which I dropped in the soup. Both
chubs and crayfish—all outside the trap—came for
the guts and had them clean and gone before they
hit the bottom or drifted downstream.

No waste nor want, Fishbone said when he
was talking about the bible, or anything else, for
that matter. Woods, life, weather, food, souls—it
should all close in back of you as you move through
life. Come in, go out, not a ripple left. Like a knife
through water. Like stovesmoke. No tracks, not
a wrinkle to show you were there. No waste. No
want. No bother to nobody or no thing. You be
there, he said, then you're not there. He'd smile.
We're all here because why, why? Because we're
not all there. Now you see us, then you don't.

Once I washed it out in the creek, I wrapped

the rabbit in dry grass to take back for Fishbone. He dearly loved rabbit dusted in flour and fried in bacon grease. Thick coating, crispy fried. Not his favorite thing, but one of them. Second favorite was 'coon meat, cut in chunks and fried the same way. In bacon grease. So deep it bubbled when you fried it.

Good as bear, he said. And bear was the best meat of all. Way back, when they went into the hills to start making 'shine, even before that, when there was just a frontier and a man had to clear his own land with his hands, when he could barely even *own* his own land, when he used a rifle that sparked flint and fired a round ball, even then they knew what was best. Deer were everywhere, and in a pinch they would eat deer meat. But the fat was bad, covered your lips and inside your mouth like candle wax. So they'd take deer for the hides, for buckskin, which made good clothes when it was soft and supple if it was worked up right. It was so good buckskin was shortened to just buck, and that became a rate of money. A single note was called not a dollar but a buck. Five bucks was five deer hides, stretched and salt cured.

But for meat they took bear.

Rich with good fat, clean fat, to use for cooking. Nothing, Fishbone said, absolutely nothing, tasted like biscuits fried in bear grease. It could preserve leather, help a small cut when it was rubbed on, grease a squeaking wagon wheel, and, when stored in a glass jar, would predict weather a day before it came. Sharpen a knife with liquid bear grease on the stone and you could shave hair with it after four swipes.

Best thing ever.

So I guess rabbit was third. Bear first, raccoon second, and rabbit third.

But I hadn't shot a 'coon. I'd seen them now and again. Usually on a tree limb when one of the Old Blue visiting dogs stuck them up an oak or an elm. They'd sit up there and snarl and spit at the dog. One of them, an old boar, must have weighed twenty or twenty-five pounds, maybe more, put up with it for a while, then dropped down and cleaned up on the dog, just beat the bejesus out of him, so he came running back to me and sat on my foot, bleeding a bit here and there, making a kind of small sound. Fishbone said they were water animals, 'coons, and if one of them got a dog in the water, he'd sit on his head and drown him all the way down. Drown him dead. Just hold his head underwater until it was done.

But I'd never shot one even though I had few chances for a shot. A hollow cane arrow was fine for a rabbit or grouse or squirrel but anything bigger . . . no. Not if I wanted a clean kill, a quick kill. A meat kill. Food. Raccoons were just too tough for a simple sharp stick and as for the other, bear.

Well.

Saw a stump near the creek, big old stump

maybe three feet across and six or seven feet tall. Or had been at one time. Completely torn to pieces, torn down and ripped to shreds by a bear looking for grub worms. Which I tried once because Fishbone said bears ate them and some natives ate them, but I couldn't hold one down. Too squishy and gutsy and smeary in my mouth and just made me lose it and puke everything up. I think I'd starve to death before I could actually eat a raw grub worm and hold it down. Of course I've never really starved, where I thought I was going to die of it the way some people have starved right to death. So it's hard to say for sure. But they're pretty bad. Gooey. Grub worms.

So I was looking at this stump thinking it must have been a giant bear, some kind of wild crazy demon bear, and then I saw it. Little thing, couldn't have been more than forty or fifty pounds soaking wet, tearing another stump to junk with just its front paws, digging in with claws as sharp and handy as knives, just pulling with strong front legs, ripping and pulling the old wood away like some kind of machine.

And I thought. No.

Don't shoot a sharp stick into something like that. It would come at you and the last thing you'd think was that you'd made some kind of perfect know-it-all mistake shooting a sharp stick into a bear. Last thing, while it used those claws and strong front legs to pull you to pieces like a rotten stump. Last thing. And that was a small bear.

Big one. No. Just clean bite your head off. Wouldn't even have time for that last thought about how stupid you were to shoot a sharp stick into a bear. One bite. No head.

Fishbone said before they sent him to Korea to get shot some they sent him to a place called Fort Sill in Oklahoma for training. Said it was about artillery, big guns which he never got to use because he got shot and took that ride between the two frozen dead men on the jeep hood before he got to shoot back even with a small gun, let alone the big ones. But they took him out in a kind of mountain-hilly country with other men where they watched the big cannons fire to learn how artillery works. Then farther out, miles out in the same kind of country, to see how they exploded when they hit. Place with old tanks and car bodies for targets and they just blew them all to pieces.

Had chiggers there. Mean little things that got under and inside his boots and underwear and ate on him, he said. Sores all over that itched worse than anything. Worst. And snakes, rattlers and water moccasins, in and around any pond or big puddle, and spiders all over as big as your fist.

Just not a good place.

Said he hated Fort Sill. Hated all of Oklahoma because of his time at Fort Sill. Said it was where Geronimo, the famous Apache warrior, was held prisoner until he died. Fell off a wagon that drove over him and broke his neck, they said, but Fishbone said he probably died just to get out of Fort Sill, take his spirit back to the deserts in Arizona where he was from. Like Jimmy Applecore. Where there were no chiggers and not as many snakes.

But near where they trained on the big guns was a kind of huge park, Fishbone said, where they kept animals in a kind of refuge, about as big a place as some small eastern states. The soldiers were put up in this animal refuge area in small tents, called pup-tents, sleeping on the ground, some of them said, so the chiggers could get at them and eat on them better, and make them into tougher and meaner soldiers.

Probably not quite true, Fishbone said, but it seemed to work that way just the same.

Soldiers got tougher, and maybe meaner, and hated Fort Sill a little more than they would have if they'd been inside clean buildings.

But where they were camped, near the artillery

range, there were other animals. Elk, deer, coyotes, and some buffalo. Thing is, Fishbone said, they had a lot of free time. Lower-rank soldiers weren't allowed to have strong liquor, like 'shine or whiskey, because they were told they couldn't handle it. Only officers were allowed what they called strong drink. Lower-rank soldiers were allowed beer.

That's where the trouble came from, Fishbone said. 'Shine would set you to singing, maybe, foot shuffle dancing, telling good stories, but it was too fast, hit a little too hard, for much else. Man would get a little tooted on 'shine, Fishbone said, and he was happy. Or sleeping. Or just quiet dead.

Beer was different, came on slower. Gave a man time to think on being crazy, mean, lead to fights. Led to stupid.

Something the army never understood, Fishbone said. Had all these men in tents on the ground mixed in with animals in this refuge with a lot of free time.

Brought in beer for them.

Cases of beer in brown cans. Free beer. Just no way, he said, any good could come from it.

So one afternoon, they were sitting by their tents, getting wetter and wetter on beer, when one of them pointed at a big bull buffalo standing not so far away, covered with dust and flies in the hot afternoon sun. He said that way back, before they had horses, the Native Americans would sneak up on a buffalo on foot and push a sharp stick into it and kill it for food. Either a spear, or an arrow from a bow. Still. A sharp stick.

Well.

Beer being free and what it was, sitting in crates of army-issue olive-drab cans with the word BEER written on the side of each can. Like you wouldn't know what they were if they hadn't spelled it out. And soldiers being bored and what they were, what Fishbone called the worst part of a know-it-all or thought they were, especially when they were drinking beer, nothing good could come of it. Too slow a drink to end fast, too tough a drink to end good . . .

Somebody, nobody quite remembered who, decided it would be a good idea to sharpen a stick, stagger drunkenly over to the buffalo, and try to push the stick into his side. Like the natives did, or the soldiers thought they did, before they had horses. Big old bull. Fishbone said it probably weighed just under a ton. Close on to two thousand pounds. Bull standing there, covered with dust and dirt and flies. Fishbone said he was amazed along with everybody else that the buffalo just stood there while the soldier walked up beside him. Hardly even looked at him.

Stopped there, the soldier, turned around and looked at the rest of them, and they waved him on. Drunk, all of them, drunk as lords, Fishbone said, they waved him on and he nodded, turned slowly, and jabbed the stick into the buffalo's side.

Or tried to.

Fishbone said he'd never seen anything move so fast. Faster than a striking snake, faster than a cat rolling onto his feet when he's dropped to the ground. Fast as lightning. Fast. The bull wheeled in place, just a blur, and went to hook a horn in the soldier's belly. Something made the soldier suck his stomach in, without thinking, and the hooking horn missed his gut—would have pulled it all out of him, Fishbone said, like fifteen feet of worms—and instead caught the belt. Heavy canvas ammo belt, part of his uniform, strong as iron. It wasn't about to break, and the horn twisted into it and locked it in place.

The bull took off at a dead run, slamming the soldier back and forth and up and down into the ground until he didn't look like a person anymore. Like a rag, Fishbone said. Shaking rag of loose meat and broken bones and blood and torn pieces of uniform. Just rags.

Hundred and fifty, two hundred yards the belt held, and the soldier slammed back and forth, up and down and finally shook loose. Laid there like old dirt, mucked with blood. Looked dead. The bull went back to just standing, in the dust and heat and flies. Wasn't even breathing hard.

But the soldier didn't die. They called for medics and three of them came with an ambulance and took him away, and Fishbone said he lived. Kept him in the hospital for months with pulleys and ropes and plaster casts holding everything together, and Fishbone said his brain quit working right. Went so sideways that they took him out of the army, which wasn't so bad because most of the men in that class got killed or frozen or shot some like Fishbone when they got sent to Korea.

Didn't know his own name.

Fishbone said he couldn't remember his own name for a couple of months and only then because the army doctors told him what it was and made him memorize it before they let him go. Sent him home to his family with his memorized name, and they had to feed him with a spoon. They said he couldn't hold a spoon in his own hand. And he never did remember the buffalo. All of it wiped clean out of his thinking like shaking dirt out of a rug.

Didn't happen much, but this time it did: Fishbone was wrong.

Said nothing good could come of the drunk soldier poking that buffalo with a sharp stick, but he was wrong.

Something good came from it. He told me the story and after that there was no way in god's green earth (which Fishbone said all the time: god's green earth) that I would try to shove a pointed stick—like a cane arrow—into a bear. Or a wild pig. Which brings up another thing: how can it be god's green earth when part of the earth is white, at the north and south poles, and blue in the oceans? So

I could ask Fishbone about that; aren't they part of god's earth? Of course I wouldn't. Ask him, I mean. That would just add to his thinking that I was being the worst part of a know-it-all. I didn't need that.

Saved me a lot of problems later, though, so that was some good from it. Not for the soldier. Fishbone said if the man was still alive, he was probably also still being fed with a spoon. But for me there were lots of times when I raised the bow, looking at a wild pig or a bear up in a tree where one of the Old Blue dogs put them. But I never pulled it back, never shot the arrow. And I could have, but didn't. Maybe saved me so I didn't have to memorize my name and be fed with a spoon.

Must have been tough, those natives in the old times. Fishbone says they had to be tougher than corrugated iron. And smart. He says they've found mammoth bones fifteen, twenty thousand years old, fossils big as elephants, with stone arrow and spear points stuck right in the bone. 'Course we don't know how it turned out. Maybe the same as that soldier at Fort Sill, Oklahoma. But they tried, just the same, and I don't know if I'd even try shooting an arrow into a hairy elephant.

Maybe if a person is starving.

Nobody bringing boxes of food back then.

No stores to get food from.

You shot the mammoth or bear then or you didn't eat. Sometimes I get pretty hungry. Seems like I'm always a little hungry. But there's always enough bacon grease and flour to make biscuits and gravy, always a can of beans. Always something. Fishbone said he knew a family even more back in the hills, so poor . . . dirt poor. Lived in the open under old tarps. Not tents, just open tarps. Had eight children and two grown people, he said, had nothing every day but gravy, sometimes with biscuits if they had flour, but most often not. Nothing. Just burned gravy. Ate off two planks tied to elm trees, ate standing up from plates that were old metal pie tins nailed with one roofing nail for each through the middle holding it to the plank. Had three spoons they passed around. Most of the young ate with their hands because the older ones got the spoons first. Said they were so bad off they wouldn't brush the flies off the gravy before they ate. Just scoop them up with the gravy and eat it all.

And still, with all of that, Fishbone said it was better than back in time when they might have to sit and eat bugs and be glad they had it. That back thousands of years ago, if you didn't grow it and you didn't shoot it, you didn't eat, unless you caught something crawling by.

Rough way to live. That's what Fishbone says. Rough way to live and probably nobody alive now could live that hard. But he said that with a lift in his voice, shuffle-pat of the foot, and a lift with an up-tone kind of crack in his voice so you thought . . .

You thought maybe . . .

You thought maybe if you worked at it and

thought on it and did it all just right . . .

Maybe you could live that way. Live rough.

Because . . .

Because Fishbone said.

Because when he said things that way, said them up instead of down, so your thinking went up instead of down, just that way, you thought you could maybe do anything.

Because Fishbone said.

Fifth Song: Dust Flower from a Soldier

Nothing around me but whirling dust,

    nothing ahead of me but silver must.

        Must come home to you.

           Think of you each morning-night,

                think of you wrong or right.

                Must come home to you.

           Think of you each live long day,

                think of you when I stand and pray.

                Got no home but you.

6

Treefriends

Fishbone says . . .

Was everything to me, what it meant. Just that. Fishbone says. Even when it didn't seem like he might be saying very much, was still something there. Could be like the seed in the center of a wild plum. They get ripe and sweet and you eat them, same with his talk, his songs, his shuffle-pats on the wooden porch. Good to listen to, whether or not it's sweet. Might be about a lady with a snake tattooed on her; or a fast car; or deep cold in Korea; or just a bird sitting on a limb, the way the light hits his feathers, his eye. Might be the color on the side of a fish, darting, there and gone. Stories there and gone.

Maybe just stories. But inside each of them was a seed, a pit, meant more than the story. More than just the sweet on the outside. You might not see it right away, might be thinking about the tattoo or the fast car and miss the reason, miss the part of the story-song that really counted.

Center.

It wasn't the tattoo, it was the beauty of it, what it meant. It wasn't the fast car, it was the story of Jimmy Applecore. How short his life turned out. How the money counted, and then didn't count at all. How there was a Jimmy and a Charlene and then there wasn't. Just gone. Didn't matter about the car or the money or the white lightning. The center was Jimmy just like the center was the woman, not the tattooed snake around her neck.

Had to see that. See the center of his story-songs.

That's how it started, how I started.

Started to think that way.

It wasn't the dream about the room getting bigger and bigger. Same dream over and over. It was the edge of the dream. Fishbone tried to help me see that and in the end he did. I'd see past what I was looking at, or over it, or through it, inside it.

Saw in a book the blue-haired woman sent me about Native American people in the Southwest. Hard to read, full of ideas that were just that, ideas. What this man thought or that man thought, but just that. What they thought. No real answers in the writing of the book. But there were some pictures as well, drawings that the natives had done on flat rocks, kind of scratched-in line drawings. One was a deer, easy to tell, sideways drawing of a buck deer. But on the inside of the lines of the drawing were more drawings, almost like doctor drawings of the guts of the deer. Plus it showed an arrow in the center of the chest, front shoulder, where the heart was. Arrow through the heart.

Then all the rest of the guts. How they went from the throat down into the stomach and then around and around and out the rear and at first it seemed like just that. Drawing of a deer. Somebody had taken one—with a pointed stick or arrow—and when they opened it up, they saw the guts and drew them.

Saw inside the deer.

That's what I thought at first. Just drawing the inside. But then I thought—talked to Fishbone about it—what if it was more. A deer would have been almost impossible to kill then. Too fast to run down, too quick to spear. Have to sneak up to get close before shooting it with an arrow. Anybody who got one had to be really good or really lucky, and for anybody living on roots and small rodents and maybe even snakes and lizards, like Fishbone said, a deer would be an almost unbelievable amount of food. Don't think I could eat a lizard. Maybe a snake. But not a lizard.

Two things.

First, you'd want to tell everybody about it. About shooting the deer. And so you'd draw the first part. Maybe a little bit of brag. Pride. You got close enough one way or another and you shot an arrow through the heart of a deer. Definitely something to brag about. But then when you opened the deer, you'd want to show where everything was for anybody else who shot a deer. Where the heart is. And the lungs. Showing how to do it. . . .

Not just a drawing but a graph. A map. A map of how to hunt, how to kill.

How to live in that moment, that second, when you are going to shoot a pointed stick into a deer, and if you do it wrong, you and your family might starve. But if you see this map, this drawing, and you do it right, if this drawing that goes way past just bragging, gets you to do the shot just exactly right . . .

So the drawing goes past the killing of the deer,

past the edge of that small dream and of killing this one deer, and shows more.

More.

And I knew then that the idea works on all things. That you can say or tell about something and in the open it will mean one thing but there will be an inside, another part that can mean something else, mean more. Tell more. Teach more.

So I came to know, to understand, that Fishbone wasn't just telling me stories. He was making maps for me, a way to go, to know, to learn, and I found myself doing the same thing.

To me. I would do it to myself. Teach myself. I would see more of something, a bush, a plant, an animal or bug. Where I used to see it one way, now I would see more, see inside it some way. Would think into it. Think inside it. And because of that I would know the thing I was watching better than I would have known it before. When I would just see it and not know it.

Like stovesmoke. Move around and through what I was seeing, hearing, studying like stovesmoke moving through the trees. Like Fishbone said, like he showed, like he told me when he said I moved through the woods like stovesmoke. Worked on this the same way.

Watched a spider for most of a morning. Sat in the soft morning sun and watched the spider weave an almost perfect circular web eight or ten inches across. Small gray spider, about as big as my thumbnail. The web was beautiful, thin strands in a complete circle with short cross strips to tighten it. Like it had been drawn in a plan and the spider followed the plan. Perfect.

I've seen webs like this before. Sometimes walked through them when they were stretched between two branches across a trail.

But now I was different and I squatted down to see more, learn more. Saw that the web seemed to capture bits of moisture from the air. Like dew.

Tiny drops that looked like diamonds when the light hit them from the back. The spider moved off to the side of the web, where it had a small cone-shaped tunnel.

Sat there. Watching as I did and I wondered if the spider had pride about the web, the perfect web, hung between two branches. If the spider thought that the water droplets were beautiful, jewel-like, as I did. Dawned on me then that anything that could make something that perfect, that beautiful, must know about it. Know how good, how pretty it was. Or why would they do it? Why make everything exactly perfect if you couldn't like it? Love it. Know how it looked.

So I sat there. Watched. Saw the spider make the web, took most of the morning, and when I would have gone, I stayed. Tried to think how it was for the spider, what it meant and then, and then . . .

It happened.

One bark moth, gray and spotted, came wheeling through the gap and hit the web, became tangled, struggled and wiggled so the framework of the web shook and the spider came barreling out of the cone-shaped nest, ran across the web to the moth, bit it once, which paralyzed it—with venom that powerful, I was glad spiders weren't as big as dogs—and turned the moth over and over, three or four times, wrapping it in strands of web to keep it there, hold it there, and was almost done, turning away, when a mosquito hit the web on the opposite side from the moth.

Caught.

Tangled and snagged, much smaller than the moth, but still food for the spider, who moved from the moth, ran back across the web, injected the mosquito, tied it with two quick wraps, and then left it and went back to the moth.

A thing to see, to tell Fishbone. But how did it know? How did the spider know to wrap the moth several times, the mosquito with two quick wraps, then back to the moth, which it took into his funnel home and ate while I watched? Ate it all while it moved to the mouth of the little tunnel and kept one of his four eyes, or maybe more than one, on the mosquito, which was still in the web.

Finished with the moth, having sucked the body completely dry, he threw the empty carcass out, off the web, then ran back for the mosquito body and brought it back to the nest. Tied it up to the side of the tunnel.

But didn't eat it.

Saving it for later. Maybe. Probably.

But again, it all had to be thought out. Everything he did, was doing, had to be thought of, an idea, and then followed through. A plan. He had to make a plan, think it all out, eat one bug, the moth, save the next for when he was hungry again. But not leave it out where something else could get at it. He brought the mosquito back into his tunnel, his house. Hung it up for later.

All thought out. Where to put the web up, how to build the web, how to wait and watch, how to deal with the moth, then the mosquito. How to save food. How . . .

How to think, I said to Fishbone that evening. Sitting with a cat. New cat, just showed up, purring and meowing. Kind of scraggly and beat-up, but just jumped up in Fishbone's lap and made himself to home. Or herself. Could have been either way. Hard to tell. Old Blue dog five or six was there too, down by the rocker, but he and the cat had worked things out between them and they just sat, or laid, listening. Seeming to listen except the dog was mostly asleep. Now and then twitching an eyelid half-open, then closing it slowly. Big old hound. Mostly ate and goobered spit on things when he shook his head. Spit on the walls, the ceiling boards, the stove. Big lips, big drool. But Fishbone liked him. Said he had a lot of love in him, so he was worth a little spit here and there.

He knew how to think, I said again. The spider knew things, how to work things out and make them happen. He hunted, snared with the web. He was a better hunter than me. Thought things out better than I did. Brain the size of the head of a pin, if that, and he was better than me.

Shook his head. Not better. Same as. Same as you, same as me.

Spiders, I said. Bugs. We're all the same. Not really a question this time. Just said it.

All things, all things. Have the same things to need. Food, air, kind of shelter, other things like us, so we're not alone. More food, more air, water. Doesn't matter if you're us, or a bug or a leaf on a tree.

But you're alone.

Not in myself, not in my head. Have all the people I knew, all the dogs and cats, all the air

I breathed, all the food I ate, all the beauty I've seen and still see. Got you, got this dog, this cat. Got the squirrel we're going to have for an evening meal with gravy and biscuits. Got a roof over my head . . .

But, I said.

Got life. Got a life. Same as you, same as the dog here or the cat . . .

Or the squirrel.

Same as, long nod. He had a life. It all starts and goes and it all ends. Like the moth the spider killed and ate, the mosquito, the squirrel. Pretty soon I'll go, then the worms get me.

No, I said.

Another slow nod. Then a sigh, like held air going out. Shoes moving, shuffle-pat, shuffle-pat. For sure, for sure. I'm old. I'm old past where it's supposed to go, where it's supposed to be. Sometimes I can't remember a thing itself, only the shadow of what it was. Woman, place, money, good food—just the shadow of what it was. Had a really good dog once, just good, now only remember the good that he was, good that he did. Can't remember quite how he looked, same as the forever woman, only remember how she was, how she seemed, maybe how she smelled, how the air around her moved, but not her. Quite. Almost but not quite. Only how she was in my memory.

Remember the chiggers and snakes in Fort Sill, but not hearing the men who had been drafted against their will who weren't from the country. City men, never saw a hard day, crying alone in the barracks at night. No real thought on that, how it sounded, only what it meant. First time away from home, some to die, some to live, but never able to be that thing again, that thing at home. Remember that, but not the true sound of the crying. Soft crying because they were soft and had to be hard. Had to learn to be hard. And it was hurting them to make them hard. Some of them couldn't do it.

Stood with blood running out of their noses and their rear ends. Remember all that, can feel all of that, but not quite how it sounded. Men crying. Same later in the hospital where they worked on my bullet holes from Korea. Remember that men cried but can't remember the sound of it. Same for the screams when they pulled steel out of some. Maybe me. Remember there were screams, but not how they sounded. That's gone. The true of it is gone.

Just shadows.

But they're more real in a way. Memory gets fuzzy, like smoke in wind, but the thing of it, the center of it, the body of it, stays true. Can't remember how my ma looked, only that when I got bit by a snake and wasn't supposed to live, she sat with me and wiped my temples with a soft wet rag that was a piece of little sister's diaper cloth. Remember the rag. How it felt. Cool, soft; and the sound she made, like music way off, but I can't remember a hair on her head. How she looked. Not a thing. Just the way she was, not how she looked.

Same for you. You saw the spider, the way it was, but later, when you've got years on you, only the shadow of the spider . . .

How smart it was.

How it saved its food.

How it could, and did, think.

And it will fill your brain and help you to reason, to think, to understand things you see, things you can't even dream on now. It's like having a special set of your own tools. Carry them with you all the time, wherever you go. Shadow memories, just sitting there, waiting to be used.

And I did.

Might have been thirteen then, or fourteen, maybe fifteen. Didn't matter how old I was. Only how my brain worked. How I could learn things.

Hunted with the bow and cane arrows that whole summer but didn't shoot anything big.

Squirrels, grouse, now and then a rabbit. Fish. Now and again crawfish. Saw things, saw everything I wanted to see. Saw it all clear and for sure deep, for sure. Went to studying on spiders, more spiders. They're probably the best hunters and I wanted to be a better hunter. Lot of them used webs across the trail, across any opening they found. Not all pretty, like that first one. Sometimes just a few strands stretched like a split-rail fence. Something flies through and just catches one wing on a strand, and they're all sticky, and it wiggles and wraps itself. A few spiders live in little holes in the ground with a tiny trapdoor on top, and when something walks by, it will shake a strand of web back into the hole, like a warning line, and the spider jumps out and takes it. Some spiders just stretch a kind of web between two long front legs and hang on a single web across the trail, completely still as if nothing is there, and when something walks by, it will kind of throw its web down on the target and drop in for the kill.

I turned spider.

I quit shooting things with the bow and went to trapping with the roll of wire. The bow was all right, but sometimes if the cane arrow didn't hit just right, it was kind of slow, not calm and easy. Little too much flopping. So I'd settle in for the evening with a soft camp, good fire, and before hard dark I'd put out a couple of wire snares. If I was after rabbits, I'd put the snares in a grass tunnel, where they ran all the time. Like little highways. If I was working on gray squirrels, I'd read the ground where they came off the tree to find food at night—always a little mark in the dirt where they left the tree—and go back up the tree about three feet and make a small noose with the wire, tied off to a limb. Then from the snare I'd run a long piece of small, braided fishing line back to the campsite, tied around my finger. Something hit the snare and I'd come awake, take up a small wood club, maybe a piece of firewood, one whack and done.

Stew.

Meat.

Anything more than I needed I'd take back for Fishbone when I came off the run, the circle. Might be overnight, might be two nights. Never much more. Fry the meat up with bacon grease and flour gravy, and either some biscuits or a couple of thin sliced potatoes, and have it with cold creek water to drink. Except Fishbone would sip 'shine with his food, or black coffee so strong it would near hold a spoon upright. Sometimes a little 'shine in his coffee. Just a touch. I didn't drink coffee at night, only sometimes in the morning, and never drank 'shine. Made my brain into mush and if I drank strong coffee at night, I'd stay up half the night, and pile bad dreams on things when I finally did sleep. Have green monsters. Once dreamed an alligator dragged me into the creek to stick me under a log until I softened up for him to swallow. One of the books the blue-haired lady sent me had a picture of crocodiles and said how they kept meat underwater under old logs to rot until they could swallow it whole. Read that and then drink strong coffee before you go to bed and I guarantee you're going to have bad dreams. Monsters. Crocodiles. Alligators.

After we ate, we'd sit on the porch and I would tell him about the loop I had made, the hunt, what I had seen and done and learned, try to tell him the inside of the inside of the very inside of things, try to draw not just the deer but the workings of it. The wind, how it was blowing, how the woods smelled in the morning wet, and the hot afternoon, every sound, every part of it, and he would nod, nod, and sip 'shine and shuffle his old boot on the porch boards and tell me story-songs. Stories that would fit into what I had been telling him so that it wouldn't just be about a squirrel or a rabbit or a deer I had seen, wouldn't just be about my hunt-ing, what I saw, but would mix in with when he was guiding elk hunts in the Bighorn Mountains in Wyoming not too far from where Custer and the Seventh Cavalry got wiped out. So hunting would mix with sad battles, joy mixed with misery, beauty mixed with ugly . . .

All there in my brain, in my thinking.

And I knew.

I knew.

Knew that it would not last forever. That I would go on bigger and bigger loops in the woods, longer and longer until maybe like the Old Blue hounds, I would find a different place to be, to think, to live. Or I would come back and Fishbone would be gone, would still be there, the shell, the body sitting in the chair but the inside would be gone, maybe to see Jesus or his baby sister or his ma that he couldn't remember. Gone.

Had to happen. I was always going longer and

longer, trying to see more, and it would be hard to get back if I went much farther. Had to push the edge of the dream out and out. Had to see my own life, my own self, how I would turn out and why I would become whichever way I went.

Or Fishbone would be gone. He was old, creaking old, rocking-chair old. Said once everybody he knew was gone, dead and gone. So either I would run so long there was no coming back or Fishbone would go. Away. Inside himself.

One or the other.

But not *now*.

Not just yet.

For the now we had, the very *now* that we had, we would keep eating meat fried in bacon grease with gravy and biscuits and I would talk about what I saw, and Fishbone would tell story-songs with his boots shuffle-patting on the board floor of the porch while he kept time and wove my stories into his stories. Closed his eyes and dozed into his memories so I could learn, I could be more, could grow more while he sipped 'shine and danced in his thoughts.

That was how it would stay.

For now.

Just for now.

**THE 30TH ANNIVERSARY EDITION
OF GARY PAULSEN'S *HATCHET* FEATURES
BRAND-NEW CONTENT AND IS PACKAGED
WITH A WATER-RESISTANT FAUX-LEATHER
COVER, MAKING IT READY TO TAKE
ON YOUR OWN ADVENTURES.**

PRINT AND EBOOK EDITIONS AVAILABLE
FROM SIMON & SCHUSTER BOOKS FOR YOUNG READERS
SIMONANDSCHUSTER.COM/KIDS

Gary Paulsen shares surprising true stories about what he has learned from animals, highlighting their compassion, intellect, intuition, and sense of adventure.

THREE-TIME NEWBERY HONOR AWARD–WINNING AUTHOR OF *HATCHET*

GARY PAULSEN

THIS SIDE OF WILD

"An absorbing read for animal lovers of any age."
—*Publishers Weekly*

"A delightful compilation of insightful and entertaining tales of animal wisdom."—*School Library Journal*

PRINT AND EBOOK EDITIONS AVAILABLE
From Simon & Schuster Books for Young Readers
simonandschuster.com/kids

Six kids who don't get along.

Enforced exile in a public restroom.

A badly hidden childhood toy.

GARY PAULSEN

SIX KIDS
and a
STUFFED

(Cat) →

From this unlikely combination,
the unexpected happens:
They enter as strangers . . . and leave as friends.

PRINT AND EBOOK EDITIONS AVAILABLE
From Simon & Schuster Books for Young Readers
simonandschuster.com/kids